AMERICAN CANDIDE
or Neo-Optimism

MAHENDRA SINGH

Illustrated by the Author.
Adapted from CANDIDE EN AMÉRIQUE *by*
Dr. Jacques O'Bean (Professor of American Studies
at the École normale supérieure du Rimouski) with
Additions Found in the Doctor's Laptop When
He Died at an Undisclosed Location
in the Year of Our Lord, 2011

American Candide: Or Neo-Optimism

Copyright © 2016 by Mahendra Singh

Published by Rosarium Publishing
P.O. Box 544
Greenbelt, MD 20768-0544
www.rosariumpublishing.com

International Standard Book Number: 978-0-9967692-1-1

FOR MY MOTHER AND TANTE NINI

Laughter is probably doomed to disappear.
— RAND CORPORATION REPORT, 1962

I

In Which Candide Is First Brung Up and Then Brung Down

IN THIS, THE BEST OF ALL POSSIBLE WORLDS, THINGS can only get better, perhaps even better than best. Of course, such a challenge is child's play for a citizen of the United States of Freedonia since anything is possible in the better than best of all possible nations—Freedonia!

Candide was just such a Freedonian citizen, a citizen whose only impediment to even further perfection was his vaguely French name. It was the final bequest of his parents, Caucasian welfare royalty who'd fled the maternity ward upon receiving the hospital bill. But no matter, his adoptive parents, the wealthy (though not obscenely so) Barons were above that sort of thing. They set small stock in a child's moniker, preferring instead to make do with the infantine cut of his adorable jib.

Despite her considerable girth, we can say little of Mrs. Baron. She was a reclusive woman who collected war-damaged children's dolls and kept to the shadows cast by Mr. Baron, an energetic man bristling with that rugged, Freedonian individualism which was the natural consequence of a lifetime of easy living. The easy living was easily explained: Mr. Baron had spent his entire life sucking on that bloated Government tit which he so loved to abuse to all who cared to listen. Bombs and bullets were his bread and butter, and he suffered no fools in his quest to make the Freedonian military-industrial complex even better than best and damn the expense.

The fruit of the Baron loins was sparse but sufficient: the young heir apparent, Junior Baron, and his sister, the invitingly bovine Miss Cunegonde. The entire Baron family lived an Edenic, feed-lot existence of food and drink consumed in vast quantities at all hours of the day and night. Fortunately, young Candide was blessed with the metabolic bravado of the congenitally impoverished. His slender physique and vacant good looks made him physically attractive enough to qualify as a fictional protagonist in even our shamefully image-obsessed times.

The Barons' home was a cavernous mansion ringed with electrified fences, motion-detection sensors, and a bulletproof guardhouse outfitted with the latest electronic gadgetry. Inside the guardhouse lurked an armed, vaguely menacing man of indeterminate though subliminally cozy racial origins. All of this ensured that nothing genuinely unsavory came sniffing around, for in this, the better than best of all possible worlds, it was obvious to all right-minded Freedonians that any evil-doers must hail from the worser than worst of all possible worlds. Perhaps this also explains why Mr. and Mrs. Baron spent their evenings watching the most lurid true-crime programs legally permissible on cable television. Like many Freedonians, they were casual voyeurs who enjoyed crime and punishment in inverse proportion to their chances of being exposed to either.

Mr. Baron did not hold with talkative college women in pants nor the rampant moral debauchery of the public schools nor even the fluoridated water piped into such establishments. He was a perpetually self-made man (beholden to none but the good lord, the ultimate self-made man in the Baron cosmology) and so he thought it better to hire a private tutor to home-school his children. Doctor Pangloss was an overweight, pasty-faced man who seemed to sleep in his clothes excessively and was given to perspiring profusely and talking loudly whenever Mr. Baron was about. His pedagogical methods had been gleaned from various AM radio talk-show hosts, street-corner pamphleteers, and the idle chatter of bus station loafers.

"Dear children," Doctor Pangloss would say, "always remember that although you're the freest people on Earth, there are those who hate you for that very freedom. And why is that? Because you are free while they will never be free—except to hate you. That's the difference that real freedom makes!

"Of course, we are all a bit different and rightly so, since god made us just as we are. But too much of anything different, such as being a show-off or gay pride parading, is harmful. It's better to be just a little bit different by being even more the same than certain other uppity folks we might mention. Now that's another real freedom!

"Let's say that you just met someone with a so-called higher education. Think about it … who gave this person the right to put himself above you in a land where all men are created equal? And if this person says that we're descended from monkeys and god endowed us with a congenital taste for hurling feces at one another instead of discussing the facts, why then, that's just silly. Look these people in the eye and tell them: 'OK, everyone's entitled to their facts, heck, I have facts of my own, strong ones too, but I don't have to always agree with them. Or yours.' So, children, here's a real fact—Mr. Baron is the better than best of all possible Freedonians."

"It's also a fact," the Doctor would conclude, "that everything that happens, just happens. Every cause has its cause except the First Cause, which must be First or we wouldn't call it so. Which is why on the back of every Freedonian banknote it says so in plain Freedonian: IN GOD WE TRUST. And who can improve upon that? That's right— only Freedonia, the best of all possible worlds, where things can only get even better!"

Indeed, who can argue with that? Certainly not Candide nor the two younger Barons, all of whom were convinced that Doctor Pangloss was the wisest of men. As for our own misgivings, will such half-truths wrapped around demi-lies wrapped around semi-falsifications ever make the factual grade? Or should we just re-label it all as a second-hand, slightly used truth? No matter, such subtle concerns never once entered these young people's innocent minds and so you can imagine how surprised Miss Cunegonde was when she observed Doctor Pangloss showing the handsome young pool boy, Paco, certain facts about the better than best of all possible worlds behind the swimming pool fence.

Blessed with a native flair for self-promotion, the young lady rushed off to find Candide. When they met, she blushed. Then he blushed. Then she pulled down her sweat-pants, enough to reveal a smudged ballpoint pen drawing of a Freedonian eagle embellishing her plump though shapely backside. Overwhelmed by the most urgent patriotic sentiments imaginable, Candide bent over to examine it more closely when Mr. Baron appeared.

The angry father wasted no time in idle speculation. Being a self-made man of perpetual action, his time was money. Without further reflection, Mr. Baron applied a hearty kick to Candide's backside and expelled the boy from the only home he had ever known.

II
In Which Candide Learns to Be All That He Can Be

THE LUCKLESS CANDIDE WANDERED FREEDONIA for a long time, homeless, hungry, and cold in the better than best of all possible worlds, a world in which the possibilities of being well-fed and warm seemed to have been unfairly monopolized by college-boy sissies. The education that Doctor Pangloss had furnished him was deficient in those obstinate facts which allow a young man to make an honest living, and naturally, that was the only sort of living that our hero would contemplate.

One morning, as the snow fell upon his shivering frame without hindrance, he took up his position beside a busy highway. Dressed in tattered clothes, unshaven, and unwashed, he brandished a small piece of cardboard upon which he had written this terse summary of his dilemma: WILL WORK FOR FOOD—GOD BLESS YOU AND THANK YOU AND HAVE A NICE DAY.

The young man darted between the cars idling in the morning's rush-hour traffic, soliciting spare change from their occupants with little success. Eventually a white van slowed down beside him, and its driver rolled down his window to examine Candide and his sign more carefully.

"God bless you and have a nice day," he exclaimed to his companion sitting beside him. "Now that's what I call a can-do attitude! This young man's starving to death in the heart of the richest nation on Earth, and he still has the good manners to say thank you."

He opened the door of his vehicle and motioned Candide to get in. A few minutes later, they were sitting inside a warm, cheerful restaurant, the two men enjoying their coffee while Candide devoured the immense breakfast of steak and eggs that his benefactors had ordered for him. Only when he was finished did he speak.

"Thanks for ordering my breakfast," he said, "but I'm afraid that I don't have the money to pay for it."

"That's OK," replied one of the men. "We could see that you were down on your luck and what caught our eye was your old-fashioned, down-home sense of courtesy about it. Most folks just curse and carry on when things go against them, but you took it like a man."

"Heck, he took it like a he-man," added his companion.

"That's my thinking exactly, he's a he-man, a real he-man," continued the first man. "Say, son, you don't have a criminal record, do you? Any problems with the law?"

"Of course not," replied Candide proudly. "I'm a law-abiding citizen. All I did was try to kiss Miss Cunegonde's backside without marrying her or even dating her first."

The two men exchanged glances over their coffee. "A real hot one, is she, Miss Cunegonde?" said one.

"Yeah, I guess so," replied Candide.

"Then I'll bet she really likes her men to be real he-men, probably he-men like you," continued the man.

"Heck, I'll tell you what she'd like even more than that," said his companion. "A man in uniform. All the really hot girls dig that. And since you're a he-man already, the uniform will just make it better."

"You're right," exclaimed Candide, quite impressed by these men's insights into Miss Cunegonde's psyche. "With a uniform, I would be—better than best!"

One of the men pushed a piece of paper and a pen toward him.

"Just sign here, son," said the man, "and you can become a real, live, better than best Freedonian hero. Heck, I cannot imagine any woman in the world who could hold out for too long against a man in the uniform of the Freedonian Army."

"Frankly, since you're a real he-man already, she'd be double-plus more unlikely to say no to you," remarked the other man. "It's like you're wearing a twenty-four-seven, rock-and-roll sex uniform all the time, and, hey, it gets even better because—"

"Wait, let me tell him this part," interrupted the other man, "because it's so darn cool, it's the best part, son—you're also going to be fighting for freedom! You see, outside of Freedonia the world is a very dangerous place to be in. It's full of angry, crazy people who can't handle the freedom we gave them already, and frankly, it's only he-men like you who can keep older, weaker guys like us and super hot girls like Miss Cunegonde feeling really safe, especially at night if you catch my drift ... stud."

"Wow," replied Candide, "where do I sign?"

The two men showed him, and the youth did so. In an instant, they bundled him back into their van and drove him to a nearby military base where he was inducted into the Freedonian Armed Forces within seconds.

After a few weeks of training and marching and shooting, Candide and several thousand other Freedonian youth were deemed ready to defend their nation. They were quick-marched to the runway of a nearby Air Force base where they stood in formation while their congressman made a few inspirational remarks. He praised their can-do spirit and even confessed to secretly envying them, for he'd been too self-absorbed at their age to join the armed forces in Vietnam when encouraged to do so by the Freedonian government.

The speech finished, all the soldiers were marched into the holds of the enormous aircraft parked behind them. To Candide's surprise, each airplane was discreetly emblazoned with the logo of Baron Incorporated. This sudden reminder that

Miss Cunegonde was linked in some way to the great adventure he was embarking upon made Candide's heart swell with love.

And then he felt a certain pride in knowing that a man so patently unjust as Mr. Baron also possessed a balancing measure of innate Freedonian fairness, at least enough to make sure that Candide would be leaving Freedonia on the better than best of all possible aircraft. Bemused by the natural justice implicit in the Freedonian notion of keeping things just as they are, Candide soon fell asleep, and, when he awoke several hours later, he was being hurried off the airplane. They had arrived in the landlocked, desert nation of Funkistan.

The next day, Candide was posted to the most remote part of this truly remote country, defending the freedom of a village so mentally and physically impoverished that even the Funkistani government did not bother to extort money or forced labor from the inhabitants.

The men of this village held their women accountable for this decline in their fortunes (several centuries ago, they had been the extorting government) and had perfected a religious system of wife beatings, dowry murder, and gang rape to redress things. When Candide complained of this to his commander, he was sent to an even more remote outpost in the desert where the tribesmen made war by rolling their Freedonian-supplied, multi-million dollar fighter planes downhill at each other. When Candide complained of this waste of the Freedonian taxpayer's money, he was sent to another outpost so desolate that it was not even populated by human beings, only by vast herds of sheep and the sheep-like, bipedal creatures who followed them about the barren landscape. At least they have religion, explained his commander when Candide remarked upon the utter futility of the Freedonian presence here.

It was here that Candide participated in Operation Unleash Freedom, the Army's mid-priced fall offensive against the terrorists who were skulking in the mountains, making life miserable for Freedonians, Funkistanis, and themselves. While defending a potato field from the enemy—a field which the enemy knew to be the private opium farm of the Freedonian-educated president of Funkistan—Candide was knocked unconscious by an explosion.

III

In Which Candide Cheats Death in the Marketplace of Ideas

WHEN CANDIDE REGAINED HIS SENSES HE FOUND himself lying upon the ground, spattered with the remains of the explosives-laden suicide bomber who had annihilated his patrol. Shaken and confused, he staggered away from the bloody scene and just in time—the entire Freedonian Army had arrived, thirsting for vengeance. Its thirst was slaked with a biblical deluge of explosions delivered upon the Funkistani landscape with a heroic disregard for the cost of it all. Hundreds of thousands of projectiles erupted, sizzled, howled, and slashed at the countryside, each one precision-guided to avoid collateral damage to innocent oil wells and pipelines. Although Candide was too terrified to notice such details, much of this uproar was inflicted upon the Funkistani nation by Baron Incorporated as part of its Freedom-Is-Free®, end-of-year, inventory clear-out.

The enemy responded by moving across the international frontier to a nearby country for a brief holiday, a cunning tactic of such novel proportions that the entire Freedonian military apparatus was dumbfounded into a sullen, hair-trigger stupor. Impressed by the enemy's tactical aplomb, Candide also fled the battle zone, disguised in the clothes of a Freedonian journalist who had succumbed to a bottle of Funkistani scotch during a lull in the fighting.

With the aid of the journalist's credit card, Candide made his way from the dark ages of the Funkistani countryside to the medieval trash heap of the Funkistani capital city. Fearful of detection by the military police, Candide adopted the Funkistani fashion of dressing in rags and even made himself a false artificial leg so that he could more perfectly play the part of a colorful refugee, a petty deception which earned him a few pennies each day from charitable Funkistanis and Freedonian photojournalists on deadline.

Unfortunately for the young man, this was most definitely not the better than best of all possible worlds, perhaps not even a possible world at all in the usual sense of things. When his credit card and begging bowl had been detained for further questioning by a Funkistani Army checkpoint (financed by a restaurateur brother of the president) our hero learned to warm himself during the cold desert nights with nothing more than his amorous memories of Miss Cunegonde.

He was sitting in a dusty, trash-littered park one morning when a crowd of Funkistanis began to gather around a large, bearded man who was shouting and waving his arms while standing beneath a disheveled palm tree swarming with dust-colored rats.

"Our beloved Funkistan cries out for freedom," shouted the man. "Long live freedom!"

Ah, a patriot whose hunger for freedom cannot be stifled any longer by a repressive and corrupt government, thought Candide.

"Death to all foreigners, infidels, blasphemers, apostates, homosexuals, journalists, divorced women, actresses, musicians, novelists, dancers, artists, single mothers, hairdressers, newspaper cartoonists, drug addicts, drunkards, prostitutes, barbers, hotel desk clerks, and female television news announcers," shouted the man. "May god give us the precious freedom to kill them all in a very short time!"

This puzzled Candide. "Doctor Pangloss once said that freedom's just another word for nothing left to lose unless you're too lazy or stupid to not even have nothing."

The bearded man glared at Candide.

"You are a fool, but I shall teach you, god willing. From where does everything come? From god since he is everything. But he cannot be evil for he is perfectly good. This is a fact—and it proves that everything evil in this world must come from those degenerates and infidels who deny that god exists."

Candide was impressed by the logic of this argument, but then another large, bearded man began shouting.

"Everyone is jealous of Funkistan because our freedom is better than theirs. We still have the freedom to believe in god without being told that we are descended from monkeys, which is so stupid an idea that not even a monkey would believe it. In Funkistan, even the monkeys are smarter than the foreign atheists." The man punctuated his speech by hooting loudly, as if imitating the monkeys mocking the atheists.

Most of the crowd joined in, although a number of large, clean-shaven men sprinkled amongst them seemed undecided.

"What foolishness, listen to me," shouted another bearded man. He wore thick, black-rimmed glasses, an indication of literacy or of having a literate hostage. "We must act quickly. My cousin, who is in Freedonia studying on a scholarship, has told me that these foreign infidels are hoping to replace our true monotheistic god with their false monotheistic god, thinking that no one will notice the difference."

Candide was shocked to hear this and could not remain silent any longer. His young heart swelled with indignation at these false accusations, the result of anti-Freedonian propaganda, no doubt.

"Dudes, you have nothing to fear from Freedonia, we're on your side," he announced. "It's so cool, how people all over the world are so much alike—"

At that moment the large, clean-shaven men revealed themselves to be the secret police by thrashing everyone else with a methodical, practiced thoroughness. It was impossible for Candide to escape their professional attentions. A large, clean-shaven man with enormous muscles hit him in the head with a riot baton which our hero recognized as Baron Incorporated's best-selling Just-Move-Along® model. Candide managed a weak, fleeting smile while he contemplated this latest, unexpected connection between his present difficulties and the woman he loved. His thoughts were cut short by another large, clean-shaven man who began expertly throttling him with his wiry hands. Our young hero's future prospects were dimming rapidly when a quick-thinking stranger snatched him by his shabby collar and dragged him to safety.

The stranger took him to a nearby house where he introduced himself as Chuck, an undercover Freedonian missionary. In short order, the energetic Chuck fed, bathed, and clothed Candide. He then gave him a small sum of money and proposed that the young man join him in his surreptitious enterprise of smuggling the Freedonian way of life to the oppressed people of Funkistan. Overwhelmed by Chuck's generosity and honored to be associated with such a humanitarian enterprise, Candide gladly accepted.

"Thanks, Chuck," he said. "You just proved to me that even in Funkistan, a Freedonian can't help but be even better than best!"

"Heck, you can't be a Freedonian if you aren't," chuckled the missionary. "Just don't leave the house for now, OK?"

The next day, Candide was looking out the window of his room when he saw a beggar on the street, an abnormally pale and hairless man of skeletal thinness, shivering in his filthy rags and drooling as he muttered to himself.

IV

In Which Candide's Love Hurts

MOVED BY THIS PITIFUL SIGHT, CANDIDE SLIPPED outside and gave the unfortunate beggar the twenty dollars that Chuck had given him. The man looked at him in surprise and then flung himself at the startled youth.

"Gee, Candide," he exclaimed between his sobs, "don't you remember your old tutor, Doctor Pangloss?"

"Is that you, Doctor Pangloss?" replied Candide. "How did you get here? Why aren't you back home with Miss Cunegonde, the hottest babe in all of Freedonia?"

The exhausted Doctor Pangloss could not reply; he had fainted of hunger. In despair, Candide carried him back to Chuck's house, where he found him something to eat and drink. After a few minutes, the Doctor had revived enough to answer Candide's questions.

"I'm sorry, Candide, but Miss Cunegonde is dead!" he announced.

Candide was so shocked by this that he fainted. Chuck, who had been listening to their conversation, revived him with a spoonful of Funkistani cough syrup.

"Miss Cunegonde is dead?" asked Candide when he regained consciousness. "I can't believe it. Did she die of a broken heart when she saw me get kicked out of the house?"

"Unfortunately not," replied Doctor Pangloss. "She was torn to pieces by a gang of bored South American dope fiends out on parole while awaiting deportation. To them, Miss Cunegonde was nothing more than a brief, blonde, and violent sexual interlude in an illicit Freedonian sojourn."

"Wow," said Chuck.

Candide said nothing, having fainted again. When he awoke, Doctor Pangloss resumed his story.

"You remember how Mr. and Mrs. Baron spent their evenings watching real-crime TV shows at home? One night, while they were watching a particularly deafening televisual re-creation of a home invasion, a gang of drugged and illegal aliens broke into their house. The noises of one crime spree canceled out the noises of the other crime spree—they never had a chance. The security officer patrolling the area had been rendered unconscious by a massive dose of prescription painkillers surreptitiously administered to him by the gangbangers. I barely survived its toxic effects myself."

Doctor Pangloss paused while Candide wept.

"Mr. Baron was shot to pieces by his private arsenal of automatic weapons, Mrs. Baron was fatally clubbed with her collection of war-damaged dolls, and Junior Baron was stomped to death like a white cockroach."

"But what's happened to you, Doctor Pangloss?" asked Candide. "You seem ... diseased in some way."

"It was that pool boy, Paco, who proved my downfall," said the Doctor. "You see, Candide ... I'm a sinner ... but now god's given me a second chance because—well, he just has to, I guess. Plus, this way he can prove that even the AIDS virus is part of his overall plan for the human race. Paco's particular strain of it almost killed me, but thanks to modern Freedonian medicine, I'm OK, in the sense that when I can afford my modern Freedonian medicine, I'm OK."

Candide was confused by this startling revelation from his beloved tutor. "Doctor Pangloss, you could really go to hell for this."

The Doctor sighed. "Apparently, yes. Sodomy between consenting, non-clerical adults is forbidden by all the world's great religions and even by some of the not-so-great ones. But don't worry, I'm still trying really hard to better myself."

"Better than best yourself, you mean," noted Candide.

"Why not, anything's possible these days," replied the Doctor.

"You could have sex with a very ugly pool boy, kind of get yourself … scared straight," remarked Chuck thoughtfully. "If sinning a lot is just a way of trying to be a better person, then a confirmed sinner like you should be on the way up, eventually."

"That could well be," said the Doctor. "I guess I'm just a really deep heterosexual with surface issues. Kind of like, I'm OK but you're more OK. Thanks for the advice, Chuck."

"Glad to be of help," replied the smiling missionary. "And now, guys, if you have nothing better to do, it's time we got to work."

He gave Doctor Pangloss and Candide a shoebox full of stuffed condoms, reminding them that each condom they swallowed would probably save an unborn fetus from certain death. Chuck also gave both men some cash, false passports, and one-way airplane tickets to Freedonia.

The next day all three men were sitting comfortably in an airplane that was orbiting the Freedonian metropolis of Hooterville, awaiting its turn to land at the international airport.

Doctor Pangloss gestured at the city outside their windows as they began their final descent. He drew their attention to the city's immense skyscrapers, vast warehouses, busy highways, and gigantic shopping malls, all of them proof positive of the economic and spiritual well-being of Freedonia.

"Even the poorest man can make his fortune here, if he's got enough of that good old-fashioned, down-home, rugged individualism," he noted proudly.

"You bet," said Chuck. "And each condom we smuggle out of Funkistan will save another precious Funkistani baby so that one day, that Funkistani baby will grow up to illegally emigrate to Hooterville and become a millionaire. Heck, he could even become an illegal billionaire. You give those people a taste of real opportunity, and they'll work like animals, unlike our native-born Freedonians who are always looking for handouts and cheap thrills. And remember, no using the washroom till we land and get to the hotel."

"I never thought of it that way," replied Candide. "Look, we're landing."

And so they were, descending into a hurricane of pitch-black clouds, howling winds, and torrential rain which had just arrived from the nearby Gulf of Mexico to pummel the city of Hooterville.

V
In Which God Makes a Fresh Start of Things in Hooterville

BOTH CHUCK'S AND THE DOCTOR'S ENTHUSIASM for the material and spiritual perfection of Hooterville was about to be sorely tested. How could they have known from an altitude of 20,000 feet that the city was mostly inhabited by the impoverished and demoralized descendants of African slaves? The affluent descendants of these slaves' former owners were too polite to harp upon the subject, but they felt that the federally mandated evolution of their property into human beings had been insufficiently appreciated by the latter. This lingering ingratitude stuck in the well-heeled craws of the upper middle class (as the very richest Freedonians preferred to be known), and so, when the entire city was casually destroyed that night by a passing hurricane, no one was too surprised.

The winds howled, the clouds unleashed a torrential rain, and the fetid waters of an entire ocean climbed over the heads of those surviving Hootervillains too patently lazy to live on higher ground. When dawn broke at last, a mighty flotilla of rescue aircraft appeared above the shattered city, an aerial armada of transport planes and helicopters flying directly overhead the mangled wreckage of the aircraft where Candide and the Doctor had taken shelter. They were the sole survivors of the aircraft's doomed landing; the other passengers had been instantly vaporized in the fireball. Their benefactor, Chuck, had ignored the usual safety procedures of an impending crash landing to station himself in the lavatory, ready to offer spiritual succor to whomever needed it most urgently, a fatal decision on his part.

"Look, they're coming to rescue us," announced Candide. As the aircraft vanished, the young man's face fell.

"Probably a bureaucratic mix-up. Those government pencil pushers are always stabbing the real heroes in the back, gosh darn 'em," sighed Doctor Pangloss. He peered into the distance. Some men were picking their way through the tangled remains of the airport terminal.

"Hey, guys, over here," shouted Candide, waving his arms to attract their rescuers' notice. Candide and the Doctor were quickly surrounded by twenty crew-cut men clad in wraparound sunglasses, tight black T-shirts, and baggy camouflage pants. They were extraordinarily muscular, their heads, necks, and torsos seamlessly blended into a monolith of engorged, steroidal flesh. Each man carried a submachine gun in his brawny hands.

"Boy, are we glad to see you," said Candide. "We just escaped from Funkistan, but our plane crashed in the storm. Thank god we made it to Freedonia. We nearly died."

"Freedonia, yeah!" said one man as he and his comrades flipped Candide and the Doctor onto the ground and bound their wrists together with plastic ties.

"Booyah," grunted another man. All of the men raised their beefy, tattooed arms to slap each other's hands while leaping into the air and yipping oddly. "Booyah," they barked in unison, clearly pleased by their expert, *en masse* subjugation of two unarmed and exhausted strangers.

"Are you the police?" asked Candide, impressed by their optimism in the midst of such devastation.

"Rah! Ooh! We're better than best police!" said one of them. "We're Tender-Mercynaries® from Baron Incorporated, booyah, and this is a federally-restricted emergency disaster area, yoot-yoot rah booh!"

"Ooh-rah, booyah," yipped his associates happily.

"But we haven't done anything," protested Doctor Pangloss.

"Not yet, hooh-yeah," laughed the man, who then kicked him in the stomach for emphasis.

Doctor Pangloss did not reply to this; he'd been suddenly gripped by the most painful stomach cramps. He slipped down his trousers and defecated. A string of stuffed condoms slithered out of him. Scratching his close-cropped head thoughtfully, the man kicked Candide in his stomach. A moment later Candide was also overcome by a similar gastric distress and expelled a perplexing heap of the same disgusting objects. Despite his discomfort, Candide forced himself to smile, knowing that he had just saved untold Funkistani fetal souls from potential death.

"Booyah!" said the man.

"Ooh-rah!" said his colleague, who nudged the condoms with the toe of his boot. One of them burst open and a quantity of white powder oozed out.

"Ooh-rah booyah," yipped the other men as they pumped their clenched fists in the air and wriggled their groins at each other.

What happened next was unclear to Candide and Doctor Pangloss for their captors had slipped black, cloth hoods over their heads and were dragging them toward a small, unmarked corporate jet sitting on the opposite end of the airport runway, fueled and ready for just such an eventuality.

VI
How Candide and Doctor Pangloss
Faced Facts Together

NO ONE HAD EVER DESTROYED A FREEDONIAN
city in one night without suffering the conse-
quences. Unfortunately for the Freedonian government, its retaliatory options were limited. The
offending hurricane was clearly an act of god, and
the Freedonian government prided itself on its
special relationship with god. It was decided—
at the very highest echelons—to put it out that
the hurricane was really Hooterville's fault and
to focus instead on the possibility that foreign
terrorists might take advantage of the confused
situation to wreak even worse havoc on the better
than best nation on earth.

Candide's and the Doctor's false passports,
Funkistani antecedents, and narcotic bodily wastes

could not fool a child. Quite frankly, the facts didn't jibe, and our heroes' muffled explanations only made things worse for them. When their hoods were removed twenty-four hours later, they found themselves in a windowless, soundproofed room.

A man in an anonymous military uniform asked the Doctor to identify the terrorist organization that had sent him to Freedonia. The Doctor's explanation was inadequate, even laughable, judging by his interrogator's sense of comic timing as he increased the voltage of the car battery attached to the Doctor's testicles.

Another man, who was sitting atop Candide and thrusting a thick, rubber hose into his mouth, asked him how he planned to destroy the Freedonian way of life. After several gallons of water had been poured into Candide, he screamed for a while but then smiled (mentally, one must admit) as he thought of Doctor Pangloss' long-ago admonition to beware of facts.

Facts! Everyone knows at least a few; but they rarely get along with your best intentions, and they're never around when you most need them. Our heroes' interrogators clearly wanted some in the worst way, and yet, every time a fact showed up, they grew even angrier. During a brief intermission between the car battery and the phosphoric acid, Doctor Pangloss tried to straighten things out.

"I'm a Freedonian citizen, and I'd like to speak to my attorney," he said. His interrogators laughed heartily at this, most of them were attorneys. One of them laughed so hard that he dropped a fluorescent light bulb into the Doctor's rectum.

"Look, guys, I hate to say this but the fact is, you've made a mistake," the Doctor continued. "We're all Freedonians here so we know that not all facts are equal and that sometimes things happen just because things happen and this happens to be one of those happening things: we're here because you're here and you're here because we're here and—"

Unfortunately, the video camera recording the Doctor's confession malfunctioned at that moment. By the time the machine had been restarted, it was too late. Those had been the Doctor's last words upon the subject of facts. He convulsed a few times and died. One of the men hastily taped an IV drip to his arm, threw a body bag over him, and wheeled him out of the room.

Candide had little more to add to his tutor's confession, despite the encouragement of the man operating the video camera. He had been lightly sodomized and beaten and even urinated upon, but his innermost Freedonian convictions had not been too badly shaken.

"Dude, I'm a Freedonian, just like you. I don't even know what's going on here," he said. "I'm not a terrorist, heck, how can I be a terrorist when I'm an ordinary Freedonian already?"

At length his interrogators grew weary of this. After a brief discussion amongst themselves in which the words 'genuine Freedonian idiot' were liberally bandied about, the black hood was replaced over Candide's head. He was frog marched through an interminable corridor and tossed into a milk delivery van full of plainclothesmen. They drove in silence for several minutes.

When they came to a stop, the hood was snatched away from Candide's head. It was very hot, and the intense sunlight was blinding. Parrots could be heard chattering amidst the lush thickets of bougainvillea and palm trees in the distance. He appeared to be in the outskirts of a tropical city. One of the plainclothesmen opened the milk van's door and pushed Candide onto the sidewalk.

"And don't do it again," he reminded our hero before driving off.

Candide decided to lie still for a while. The few pedestrians gingerly edging their way around him studiously ignored this bleeding and bruised human wreck until an old woman crept up to him and said, "Be brave, gringo, and come with me."

VII
In Which Candide Gets Lucky

CANDIDE FOLLOWED THE OLD WOMAN TO A decrepit hovel beside a trash dump. The hovel and the trash dump were indistinguishable from each other, but Candide was no longer very fussy about such things. He collapsed onto a mattress constructed from discarded fast food containers and nibbled a bit of the expired Freedonian spam that the woman offered him. When he had finished eating, she gave him some ointment for his injuries.

"Apply this to your wounds and go to sleep. I'll return tomorrow," she said.

"Who are you?" asked Candide. "Why are you doing this? And where am I, anyway?"

"You are in the Republic of Costaguana," she replied and left.

Gosh! Costaguana! Whatever will they think of next? thought Candide, quite amazed at this turn of events. He fell asleep, and, when he awoke the next morning, the woman had returned with a second-hand enchilada and another tube of ointment. She inspected his wounds, made certain he ate properly, and left him to sleep again.

After three days of this, Candide was feeling much better. When the woman returned in the evening, she was pleased to see that he was fully recovered, thanks in no small part to his innate Freedonian sense of a perpetual, god-given well-being beyond the ken of ordinary mortals.

"Thank you for saving my life, ma'am," he said. "I always thought Costaguana was a violent, Latin American banana republic run by drug dealers and thugs, but you sure showed me wrong. It turns out that Costaguanans are the nicest, friendliest foreigners on earth."

The old woman looked at him warily. "You're welcome, Freedonian gringo," she replied, "but now you must be quiet and come with me again." She took him by the hand and led him outside into the humid tropical night. They hurried down a deserted country road until they reached an industrial park of warehouses surrounded by a tall, cyclone fence topped with concertina wire. They followed the fence, taking care to stay in the shadows until they discovered a man-sized hole that someone had cut in the fence.

They slipped through it and crept past the warehouses, cautiously making their way toward the nondescript trailer that lay in the center of the industrial park. The woman knocked on its door and, without waiting for a reply, opened it and motioned Candide to enter.

The trailer was splendidly furnished inside with wall-to-wall, red shag carpeting, red velour wallpaper, and plush, scarlet curtains embellished with gold embroidery. A heart-shaped, pink waterbed filled the center of the trailer, and the mirrored ceiling above the bed underscored the festive, if dizzying, carnal ambience.

"Dude," murmured Candide.

The woman told him to sit on the bed and vanished into another room. When she returned, she was supporting, with great difficulty, a young woman who seemed unable to stand up on her own. The woman was well-upholstered, blonde, and attractive in a nonthreatening, bovine sort of way. Except for her mirrored sunglasses, fishnet hose, platform shoes, and the usual tattooed graffiti of modern Freedonian youth culture, she was entirely naked.

"Go ahead, gringo," sniggered the old woman, "take it off. Take it all off."

Consumed with curiosity, our young hero stood up and removed the woman's sunglasses. He staggered backwards. He fainted. He fell onto the bed. It was none other than Miss Cunegonde—and she too had staggered backwards, she too had fainted, and fallen onto the very same waterbed—right beside Candide!

The old woman revived both of them with a few spoonfuls of Costaguanan cough syrup. When they had recovered sufficiently from their surprise, they began to speak.

"Wow, is that really you, Miss Cunegonde?" asked Candide. "I thought you died after being molested in every possible way by drug-crazed, illegal alien sex fiends who tore you limb from limb in their animal lust."

"Yeah, I guess so," admitted Miss Cunegonde. "I'm a survivor."

"But what about Mr. and Mrs. Baron? And Junior Baron?"

"It was a really bad scene, Candide," she replied. She gazed blankly at him for a while.

"Whoa," said Candide.

"Yeah," replied Miss Cunegonde.

With their carnal passions now inflamed to the highest possible degree that can be safely tolerated by modern youth, they fell upon each other and had premarital sex. After they had finished, Candide told Miss Cunegonde the story of his adventures in Freedonia, Funkistan, and Costaguana, not forgetting to include the tragic fates of the missionary Chuck, Doctor Pangloss, and the entire population of Hooterville.

"Man, that's pretty heavy," said Miss Cunegonde. "It's like we've both been separated and had a really ... rough ... time. Hey, do you want to hear my story?"

He certainly did. And while she spoke, the young Candide devoured her with his eyes the entire time. She wasn't just hot—she was better than best hot!

VIII
In Which Miss Cunegonde
Has an Awesome Flashback

"After the illegal aliens raped me and killed everyone else in the house, they took me with them on their crime spree, and, since they were already illegal aliens, everything they did to me during their crime spree was even more illegal. I couldn't take it any longer, which is probably why they sold me to a man in the adult video business for five kilos of Costaguanan cocaine. It's kind of flattering when you think about it."

Candide did think about it and was suitably impressed.

"Wow."

"Yeah, huh?" she agreed. "His name was Dirk, and he had an MBA from a real Ivy League university. He explained everything to me. Apparently, what I would be doing for him was really pretty smart. I would be monetizing my only asset, and, since my only asset was a natural, renewable, local resource, it would all be *green*.

"Anyway, working for Dirk was OK until he lost a lot of money in the stock market thanks to nosy government regulators who couldn't stand seeing businessmen like Dirk get rich just by making their money work harder than most other human beings could ever possibly work. Plus they were jealous of Dirk getting to hang out with me and some other really hot girls in those sexy videos we made for other rich businessmen who work so hard that their wives don't even have time for them anymore."

"That's so unfair," interrupted Candide, "but what can you expect from people who weren't home-schooled by Doctor Pangloss?"

"Not much, apparently," said the girl. "Luckily for Dirk, one of his fraternity brothers had what they call a 'brainstorm,' and he packaged me and the rest of Dirk's girls into pre-leveraged, asset-backed AAA-rated securities which they then collaterized into refinancing Dirk's margin calls on his FOREX trades, whatever that means."

"Only in Freedonia," agreed Candide, who understood nothing of this.

"Yeah, huh? Dirk was so upset that his buddy practically had to force him to do it, he even started crying when he had to sign the papers, but he was so brave about it that afterwards everybody voted to put him in charge of those nosy, jealous government regulators and make them stop harassing defenseless people just because they're rich."

"Whoa," agreed Candide.

"Yeah, whoa, huh?" she replied. "That's when another fraternity brother of Dirk had an even bigger brainstorm and managed to write me off as a capital loss, which is how I wound up in Costaguana, I guess."

"All the way to Costaguana—just like me!" said Candide.

"Yeah, it's kind of surreal, huh?" giggled Miss Cunegonde. "And Señor Armando is really sweet. He even fixed up this trailer for me to stay in while he's busy all night figuring out ways to smuggle stuff from Costaguana to all those Freedonians too poor to travel here and get it on their own. All of those warehouses outside are full of his ... *stuff* ... I think.

"During the day, he's also really Colonel Armando from the Costaguanan State Security Forces, and since the Colonel's busy all day figuring out ways to stop smugglers like Señor Armando from destroying Freedonia with their Costaguanan stuff at night, well, they've both been under a lot of stress recently. Between one Armando and another, I don't get much time off. I work pretty much twenty-four-seven, three-sixty-five, round-the-clock."

"You always had the nicest handwriting," said Candide.

"Right, huh? Because one night I was watching TV, and I freaked out because there was Doctor Pangloss. He'd become a terrorist, and they had videotaped his confession. It was really creepy. He kept saying over and over: I'm a Freedonian ... and ... I hate ... Freedonians ... because you're here."

"That's so not true!" said Candide heatedly. "Doctor Pangloss died because he loved Freedonia too much. I know because I was there!"

Miss Cunegonde smiled at Candide. "Yeah. They also had a video of you confessing. You looked cute for a terrorist."

Candide hastened to explain that both his

and Doctor Pangloss's confessions had been extracted from them under duress approaching (although not exceeding) the pain experienced by the average Freedonian losing several major internal organs all at once or even the average non-Freedonian simply dying outright.

"That's so gross," she said. "But anyway, this really old, kind of creepy Costaguanan lady who helps me out with the Armandos from time to time, she volunteered to find you and bring you back to me. It was pretty awesome."

This so pleased Candide that he resolved to have even more premarital sex with Miss Cunegonde and the heck with getting married. Freedonia was far away, and the Costaguanan miasma of moral turpitude that pervaded the entire trailer and its lascivious furnishings was inescapable and irresistible. Something had to give, and, as always, clean living would have to take the brunt of it. Which is why only a Costaguanan reader will be disappointed to learn that, just as the two young Freedonians were preparing to resume their illicit embraces, the door of the trailer opened and Señor Armando appeared. It was Sunday morning, and he had arrived to enjoy his daily tryst with Miss Cunegonde.

IX

How Candide Took Out
Two Armandos for the Price of One

TANNED AND FIT WITH PERFECT HAIR, PERFECT
teeth, and perfect posture, Señor Armando was
an unsettling experience for Candide. His co-
logne was freshly made in Paris, France, and
his silk business suit had been flown in from
Europe on his private, bio-fueled jet. He spoke
five languages fluently, understood the difference
between a *terroir* and an *abattoir*, and, despite
Candide's suspicions, knew how to treat a lady.

"Darling, I thought I'd drop by without ring-
ing first—oh, I see that you have a visitor," said
Señor Armando in the elegantly accented Freedonian he had acquired at a prominent East Coast,
Freedonian prep school. He put his briefcase on

the floor next to the gently undulating waterbed and shook Candide's hand. His grip was firm and dry. He looked the young Freedonian right in the eye.

Candide was having none of this.

"Dude, you better back off," he said.

"OK, that's great, drop by another time then. The service entrance is in the back," replied Señor Armando. He smiled at Miss Cunegonde. "Listen, darling, I've spent the whole night sorting stuff into cargo containers for tomorrow's shipment to Baron Incorporated—"

The mere mention of the name Baron was the final straw for Candide's rough-hewn, masculine heart. Seizing the reins from his brain, it told him what to do in a compelling yet snappy series of vivid mental pictures. He didn't even have to think—he was probably a natural—for his specialized Freedonian Army training allowed him to snatch up the pistol laying on the nightstand and shoot Señor Armando dead, just so.

"Like, you just killed the number one narco smuggler in South America?" said Miss Cunegonde.

"Yeah. And the head of the Costaguanan State Security Services?" added Candide.

"Totally. It's like, we're in some kind of block-buster action movie and there's only one bullet but you got two revenges. Are you OK, Candide?" asked Miss Cunegonde.

Candide sighed. "It's just that, sometimes … after being kicked in the ass, thrown out of your own home, starved, frozen, blown up, beaten up, crash-landed, beaten up again, drowned, sodomized and urinated on, a man has to be a man. Especially for a Freedonian babe like you."

"Wow. Doctor Pangloss wasn't a terrorist after all," mused Miss Cunegonde. "I mean, he was right—you're becoming a better than best Freedonian."

The old woman had reappeared. She scowled at the body lying at Candide's feet.

"Damn it, boy, you're noisy and violent, and you've ruined everything," she said. "If we don't flee immediately, we'll all be tortured and killed by the Costaguanan State Security Forces. And that is nothing compared to what the narcos will be doing to us at the same time."

Without further delay, the old woman removed the dead man's wallet from his pocket. It was stuffed with crisp, newly printed Freedonian hundred dollar bills.

"That's enough for cab fare back to Freedonia," said Candide.

"You're right," said the old woman. "We'll take a cab. I'll manage somehow, sitting down for so long, even though I only have one buttock left."

By evening their taxi was racing past the international frontier as the Costaguanan border guards waved them through in a flurry of Freedonian bank notes. A few hours later they had reached the city of Pickapeppuh and checked into a hotel under the names of Mr. and Mrs. and Granny Blandser. After reminding the driver to return in the morning at eight o'clock, the weary travelers fell asleep.

As they slept, a platoon of Costaguanan Security Service paramilitaries (cunningly disguised as Costaguanan narco gangsters) was entering the Armandos' trailer. After an agonizing reappraisal of the facts by these bewildered men of action, a Freedonian military advisor took charge of the situation and swiftly resolved the embarrassing public relations problem of the two dead Armandos. A pesky *campesino* who had walked into the Security Forces' bullets that very night was promoted to the rank of international narco-terrorist Señor Armando, and in an instant, the

Republic of Costaguana had gained a hero and lost a villain.

After all, one bullet-smashed face is very much like another, as the military advisor noted in his official report to the Freedonian Central Intelligence Agency (and his unofficial report to Baron Incorporated). In any case, while the body of Colonel Armando lay in state beneath the dome of the Costaguanan Pantheon of Heroes, a festive rap video was hastily produced to commemorate the event. It featured a squadron of dope-addled Costaguanan paramilitaries masquerading as narco gunmen lasciviously rubbing at their crotches and writhing in haphazard unison around the mangled corpse of the newly-minted Señor Armando. From the paramilitaries' point of view, it was all a final, crushing insult to a hated enemy although the narcos preferred to regard it as a sentimental tribute to a fallen comrade. In any case, the video was broadcast to the grieving and slightly confused Costaguanan nation during a commercial break in the televised state funeral of their treacherously murdered crime-fighting hero, the late—and semi-fictional—Colonel Armando.

X

In Which Candide, Miss Cunegonde, and the Old Woman Improve Their Collective Bottom Line

THE NEXT MORNING, MISS CUNEGONDE JOINED Candide and the old woman in the hotel restaurant for breakfast. She was not feeling well.

"Do you remember all that money we had when we left Costaguana?" she asked. "It's really weird, but I can't remember where I put it last night."

"Damn! These Pickapepperonis are all thieves, hustlers, and con men," said the old woman. "One of them must have slipped into your room while you were in the shower and stolen our money."

"Doctor Pangloss was right," sighed Candide. "These foreign countries are all fakes. They look friendly, but everybody's a crook. And the worst ones are probably our best friends."

The old woman snorted so loudly at this that she accidentally inhaled her coffee. "Who cares? Miss Cunegonde will have to earn some more money and quickly. This hotel is full of lonely businessmen, young lady, so get busy, and we can leave by lunchtime. I'd do it even though I only have one breast left, but I'm probably too old, even for these fat gringos."

Our young hero was baffled by this talk of doing it with fat, gringo businessmen. What was *it?* He had been under the impression that Miss Cunegonde was a warehouse trailer receptionist working her way up the corporate ladder by doing great things with packaged assets and fungible securities underneath mirrored ceilings, whatever the heck that meant.

Miss Cunegonde leaned over and planted a kiss on her perplexed sweetheart's cheek. "Doctor Pangloss always said that the business of Freedonia is business," she reminded him. "That means don't do anything for free, unless you want everyone to disrespect you and call you a really cheap slut. And that kind of sucks."

Our young heroine made her way into the

hotel lounge where she soon met a Freedonian businessman enjoying a weekend sabbatical. Although Baxter had come to Pickapeppuh to sample the local scene (he had a thing for dark, slim foreign women who let themselves get noisily trapped underneath fat, white men), he was willing to say the heck with that, at least for five minutes. A hasty rendezvous was arranged for his air-conditioned hotel room on the 15th floor. Afterwards, while Baxter was tidying up in the washroom, the young woman rifled through his pants, determined to make the best of things by any means necessary. His business card soon caught her eye.

When Baxter returned to the bedroom, Miss Cunegonde was ready. "That was really fun," she sniffed, her eyes brimming with tears, "but my brother's a Freedonian war hero who just assassinated the number one drug smuggler in South America while he was trying to rape me ... again."

"Hey, that's quite a story," replied Baxter as he began dressing.

"Yeah, huh? If only my brother and I could tell it to a larger audience, before other young Freedonians like us get caught up in these dangerous, foreign, get-rich-quick schemes."

Baxter paused to think, his trousers around his ankles.

"You know what? I'm a booking agent for the practically number one-rated, comedy-news-reality show on Freedonian TV. It's called *Yeah!* ... like the word for 'yes' but more folksy, less threatening. We're always looking for real people to appear on our show."

"My brother's very real. And so is being raped by a South American drug lord."

"I bet. Why don't you send your brother up here whenever he's available? I'd love to meet him."

Miss Cunegonde rushed downstairs to give Candide the good news. An hour later, our hero rejoined his companions in the hotel lounge.

"Baxter says I'm a natural for *Yeah!*" announced the smiling youth. "He says that I'll probably test through the roof, all the way to eleven! And he gave me enough money for all three of us to fly back to Freedonia and appear on a special, live episode of *Yeah!*"

"I'm so proud of you, honey," said Miss Cunegonde. And even the old woman conceded that Candide had done very well. Both he and Miss Cunegonde had earned sufficient funds for all three of them to escape the jungle barrios of South America for the celebrity barrios of North American cable TV.

"Baxter remembered me from the Freedonian Army," he told them as they hurried to the nearest travel agency. "He was really impressed by the Rapture drone video they made of me being blown up by terrorists while defending the President of Funkistan's potato farm. He saw it on the internet."

"It really is a small world after all, huh?" said Miss Cunegonde.

"All the more reason to get out of here before the Costaguanan State Security Forces and the Costaguanan narcos arrive," warned the old woman. "Being blown up by terrorists is a cupcake compared to them."

Candide heartily agreed with her and quickly purchased three one-way tickets on the next airliner out of Pickapeppuh.

"Destination—Wollyhood!" he told the travel agent. "Thanks to the generosity of *Yeah!* I can afford to bring my girlfriend and this, uh, old woman along with me to the capital of the Freedonian entertainment industry."

"It's a twenty-hour flight," noted the old woman, "but don't worry about me, boy, even though I'm old and tired and have only one kidney left."

A few hours later they were flying high above the Pacific Ocean in a jet airplane bound for the glamorous metropolis of Wollyhood. All three of them were enjoying their in-flight meals and free, complimentary beverages when Miss Cunegonde broke a fingernail.

"Darn it," she sniffed. "My life, like, totally sucks."

"You're almost as stupid as your gringo boy-friend," replied the old woman. "Even though I only have one lung left, I still have enough sense to know that I'm far worse off than you or any woman from Freedonia, where life is so easy that even the whores die of old age."

Both Candide's and Miss Cunegonde's curios-ity was aroused by this bold pronouncement, and they begged the old woman to tell them the story of her own, far more wretched life.

XI

How the Old Woman Got Old

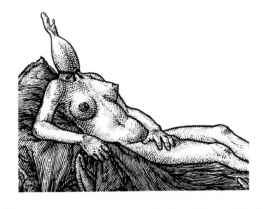

"I WAS NOT ALWAYS AN OLD WOMAN, RUDE
gringos," she said. "I began my life as a young,
voluptuous farmer's daughter from Macarena,
the colorful, yet otherwise utterly impoverished
southern neighbor of Freedonia. For years we
tried to make a living by exporting bananas to
Freedonia, but it was always the same: the money
always vanished somehow before it reached us.
We exported sugar cane to Freedonia, but that
time the check was lost in the mail. We tried
exporting coffee, animal hides, fresh strawber-
ries, and even aquarium fish, but every time the
money was eaten by a Freedonian dog or stolen
by a hopped-up drug fiend in the Freedonian
mailroom. And one time, the check was printed

with invisible ink and simply vanished from under our very eyes.

"Soon we had nothing left to export but ourselves. My firm, shapely breasts and smooth, brown thighs caught the eye of a *coyote*, a trafficker in human beings, and he persuaded my parents to export me to Freedonia. Along with several other girls, I was packed into a chicken truck heading north.

"If you've ever spent three weeks inside a Macarenan chicken truck, you'll know that heat, dust, hunger, and fear are the least of your troubles. Even now, when I have only one ovary left, I still can't be bothered to worry over such trifles. Things will always get worse, especially when every policeman, federal agent, border patrol officer, and customs official along the way has to inspect each one of your bodily orifices for illegal drugs, cash, or weapons.

"Luckily, I was just as tough then as I am now. The other girls in the truck did nothing but complain and threaten to run away; but I was a farmer's daughter from the poorest state in Macarena, and I knew that poverty was a crime, especially amongst criminals. This is because no one respects private property more than criminals, and that's also why so many of them are policemen. After thinking it over for several days, I chose the least disgusting policeman and made him fall in love with me."

The old woman simpered, looking quite pleased with herself, and took another sip of her soda pop. Candide and Miss Cunegonde were genuinely impressed with her story so far and begged her to continue.

"I've forgotten his name and his face. There's never enough light inside those chicken trucks anyway. But he seemed happy with me and even promoted me from chicken truck to hog trailer. Those were my salad days, but even back then, when I was just a young girl with both of her big toes, I knew my good luck would not last much longer.

"We had stopped one night at a remote desert filling station when a rival gang of smugglers attacked us without warning. I was in the filling station's washroom, and I heard every one of the policemen and the girls being torn limb from limb by the smugglers. These men were very dangerous and very passionate. They were armed with expensive, Freedonian automatic rifles and brand-new, German machetes, and they were determined to teach the police a lesson.

"I left the washroom when they were finished. I was the only person left alive in the filling station. Blood-soaked heaps of dead bodies surrounded me. I could not even recognize my police lover boy. The smugglers had completely disassembled him and the others and then re-arranged all of them back together at random. It was a human salsa."

The old woman shook her head and snorted loudly.

"I didn't have time for that sort of crap back then, and I still don't now. I took some candy bars from the filling station and walked back to the highway in the dark. By the time the sun had risen, I had finished my breakfast, said my prayers to the Virgin Mary, and hitched a ride with a very nice black man in a large, pink Cadillac. He was a rap star on his way to Freedonia to sign a contract with a major recording label. I had always thought that rap musicians were loud, badly-dressed men obsessed with having clumsy sex with greedy, shallow women, but this man told me that it was all a marketing ploy. In fact, he was a homosexual who preferred nothing more than a quiet evening at home, cooking a nice meal for his friends while listening to Palestrina on his hi-fi system.

"None of this made any sense to me but even in those days I expected nothing more from the world, I can tell you. Roderick told me that I could stay with him in Freedonia as long as I did one thing for him—pretend to be his girlfriend so that his other rap musician friends would not suspect the truth. What did I care? I had both of my intestines back then so I was still young and crazy, a pretty girl away from home for the first time in her life."

The old woman paused to finish her soda pop in one swallow. She wiped her mouth with the back of her hand and tore open her packet of airline peanuts with her sparse, yellow teeth.

XII
How an Old Woman Makes Ends Meet in Today's Global Economy

"I HAD FINALLY MADE IT TO FREEDONIA, THANKS to Roderick," she continued. "His house was very nice, and he treated me like a lady, which is more than I can say for most heterosexuals. But even then I knew that only the rich can afford to remain surprised by human nature in this miserable world, and, since I was not rich, I certainly was not surprised when I returned home one evening to discover that Roderick had been outed by another jealous rapper.

"You may think that narco smugglers are dangerous, but they're a baby fart compared to a full-blown Freedonian media frenzy. The TV reporters and *paparazzi* and stalkers made Roderick's life so miserable that he had to pay an enormous sum of money to a famous televangelist who had agreed to convert Roderick back to heterosexuality in front of a live studio audience of good-looking young men. Naturally, I would have to leave the house forever because once Roderick was a heterosexual rap star, he must never seem to be too monogamous. At least that's what Roderick told me as he was driving me to the bus station.

"None of that mattered because we never made it there. A disgruntled postal worker with an Army surplus sniper's rifle decided to go on a homophobic rampage at that very moment, and he killed Roderick with one shot to his head as we were driving by his mail truck. Before I could seize the steering wheel from the dead man's hands, we swerved into an oncoming school bus full of disabled children on their way to the zoo. The last thing I remember before I was pushed into the ambulance was thinking how stupid it was to make children visit a zoo when you can just drive them to their parents' offices or bedrooms and let them see the same sort of animal behavior for free. Even imbecile gringos like you will agree with me that the disgruntled postal worker probably had something similar in mind.

"They operated on me in the hospital, but, when they discovered that I was an illegal alien with no money or insurance, a man in an expensive suit came to visit me in the recovery ward. He told me that the explosion triggered by the collision of our car and the school bus had destroyed an entire city block and killed or wounded at least fifty people, far more than Roderick's auto insurance could afford. Even though I was in great pain after having half of my lungs and intestines surgically removed, I was not surprised by this. I told the man that as soon as my bandages could be moved, I would sleep with him or anyone else who needed to make money from this accident.

"Don't look so surprised, this sort of thing happens all the time and especially to me. My life is such crap that even when I die, I'll probably have to keep on living. At least I'm tough enough to take it, unlike you two. That's because I'm a Macarenan farmer's daughter, unlike that smirking gringo lawyer who didn't even have the *cojones* to do what he was really thinking. Instead, he sent me in a taxi to a hotel room where I fell asleep, and when I woke up, my backside was on fire and I had to do my business every five minutes. The taxi came back for me the next day. The driver happened to be a surgeon from the Democratic Republic of Savoy who told me that I must rest and drink plenty of fluids for the next few years, if I was lucky."

The old woman sneered at Miss Cunegonde and Candide.

"If you think that living this long after selling one of your kidneys is lucky, then you are even more foolish than you look. But then again, an extra kidney was a luxury I could never hope to afford, no matter what slack-jawed loafers like you might think. My pretty Macarenan face had been permanently scarred in the car crash so I learned to make my living in the monster porno film business. Yes, go ahead and laugh, what do I care? The men who watch such rubbish have never once bothered to look at my face, much less remember it. And why should they? Who wants such memories?

"Time has made me uglier, older, and lesser. When the movie producer replaced me with a younger and more stupid girl, I made enquiries about that surgeon from Savoy and soon found him working in a falafel stand. Thanks to him, my big toe soon found gainful employment as a sturdier sort of thumb on someone else's accidentally maimed hand. Of course, there was a bad recession right after that, and lots of people made a silly fuss over it; but for me, things were so awful already that the recession was a holiday from solitary misery to communal misery.

"I dabbled again in the export business when the surgeon from Savoy arranged for one of my ovaries to show up for work inside a 60-year-old heiress. She wanted her grotesque maternal instincts made into the subject of cocktail party gossip amongst her equally bored society friends. When that money ran out, I got a job in a store selling lawn furniture to other illegal aliens too poor to afford real furniture inside their homes.

"They don't make illegal aliens like they used to. Sleeping on lawn furniture is chicken shit compared to being so poor you can't even afford to lie down when you sleep. You try lying down, gringos, when you've had to sell your left buttock to a movie starlet who's trying to fatten up her ass in time for the Oscars. Between one thing and another, my life has been a perfect hell for as long as it took a beautiful young girl to turn into an ugly old woman. And I won't even go into the reasons why I had to sell my right breast to an airline hostess who had lost her breast implants in a sudden change of cabin air pressure.

"You'll never be worse off than me, no matter how hard you try. At least I don't have an education to confuse me and make me soft in the head like you. When I met Señor-Colonel Armando, he offered me the job of keeping an eye on Miss Cunegonde because I'm so old and ugly that most men think I'm invisible. But once I was even prettier than you, young lady.

"Maybe I'll kill myself. But then I remember how the big shots upstairs treated the Virgin Mary, leaving her pregnant and in the lurch with a suspicious husband and useless relatives. So I think I'll stay down here as long as I can, just long enough to really piss off anyone stupid enough to think that they can pull the wool over my eyes.

"Broken fingernail? Ha! I'm a broken human being."

XIII
In Which Candide Gets His Fifteen Minutes

"WHOA," SAID CANDIDE.

"I'm never going to call you an old woman again," said Miss Cunegonde.

"What do I care?" snapped the old woman. "You're a greedy tart, and your boyfriend is a waste of space; but I've been an old woman for so long that it's starting to suit me. Or perhaps I'm just getting soft in my old age."

"It's too bad that Doctor Pangloss is dead," said Candide, "because he'd probably be your number one fan right now. I mean, you're living proof that Freedonia is the better than best nation on earth. You sacrificed everything you had in Macarena just to live the Freedonian dream. That's really awesome."

The old woman did not bother to reply to this for she had fallen asleep. Candide and Miss Cunegonde also fell asleep a few minutes later, exhausted by their recent adventures. When they awoke in the morning, they were in Freedonian airspace, and the city of Wollyhood sprawled beneath their wings, resplendent in the rising sun. As soon as they landed, they were whisked away in a limousine to a small but cozy bungalow behind the *Yeah!* studio in the Wollyhood Hills. After freshening up, Candide went straight to the studio to see what was up.

The network executives at the studio were quite excited and for good reason. Baxter had cabled them, alerting them to Candide's uncanny ability to function in a state of cognitive dissonance that beggared the imagination. The amiable young lad simply thrived on wishful thinking, there was no other scientific explanation for it. He might well be able to connect with a Freedonian TV audience on such a deep, intuitive level that the marketing geniuses behind *Yeah!* did not even have a word for it yet. The main thing was to get him on air as soon as possible before *Yeah!*'s market share eroded even further.

When Candide arrived on the set, he was

whisked into a chair behind a gleaming, chrome-plated newsreader's desk flanked by towering banks of color TV screens flashing up-to-the-minute video feeds of war jets flying over burning oil wells. In the seat next to him was Chad, the preternaturally photogenic host of *Yeah!* and one of the founding fathers of the comedy-news-reality-TV genre.

Chad smiled warily at his next guest. Chad was a man wracked by internal dissension at this moment. His desire to salvage his career was neatly balanced by his intuitive loathing of this genuine specimen of Freedonian manhood sitting beside him.

Chad adjusted his tie, cleared his throat, and faced the camera. "Tonight we have with us a young Freedonian who's not only been blown up by Funkistani terrorists but was also forced to watch a Costaguanan drug lord rape his sister … over and over."

Every video screen behind them simultaneously switched to a grainy, slow-motion loop of a swarthy man menacing a blonde girl with a rubber knife. His brow furrowed with concern, Chad went to work.

"Wow … Candide, we can't even imagine

what you must have gone through … so you're going to have to tell us yourself. What exactly was going through your mind?"

Candide blinked at him. The studio lights were very bright, and his mind was an utter blank.

"OK, fair enough. Let me rephrase that. After being blown up and then having to watch your sister get raped by an illegal alien, what happened next?"

Candide gulped. His mouth was so dry. His mind remained stubbornly blank—and then he recalled what Doctor Pangloss had once said upon this very same subject, so many years ago.

"Thanks … Chad … I guess what happened to me and my, uh, sister was a pretty good example of how confused some foreigners really are about Freedonia. I mean, come on, they're either trying to kill us or have sex with us. What's up with that? I don't think they can handle the freedom we keep having to give them every few years. I think they're just jealous because—*Freedonia rocks!*"

The studio lights shining into Candide's eyes made it impossible for him to see the studio audience's reaction, but he could hear their murmured approval.

He continued, more confident now. "I'm not

ashamed of being blown up in Funkistan because that way I wouldn't have to be blown up back here in Freedonia. Besides, that's not how they trained us. They trained us to be blown up overseas. That was the mission."

"Yes, that was your mission," said Chad. "You weren't one of those phony soldiers that we keep seeing in the media nowadays, the ones who don't let themselves get blown up because it wasn't in their mission."

"The mission is the mission, man," replied Candide.

An attractive woman in the front row of the audience sighed loudly. A man bit his lips, his eyes brimming.

"Yes … the mission is the mission … very well put," continued Chad. "But what about your sister? What kind of sick, twisted, criminal mind decided that her mission was being raped?"

"Frankly, Chad, that guy was so stoned that I had to shoot him five or six times just to get him to lose his erection. They just don't think like us. That guy was an animal and—"

Candide was startled by the sudden change of imagery on the TV screens surrounding them. A video loop of a fat man in a lab coat blowing himself up with test tube chemicals was being played at a frantic speed.

Chad chuckled. "Hey, this just in from the we-can't-believe-it's-true department. Some scientists are still claiming that the earth is warming up too fast for safety. Any thoughts from a young Freedonian hero about these so-called global warmers?"

"Global warming, huh? That's stupid. How can you warm a whole globe?" replied Candide. The audience roared with laughter at the young man's down-home shrewdness.

"Only in Freedonia, apparently," grinned Chad. He handed our hero a plain brown envelope stuffed with several thousand dollars. "And here's a small token of our appreciation, just a way for us to say thanks. Thanks for helping us fight terrorism, sexual abuse, and thousands of scientists working for decades to discredit and confuse a lot of Freedonian radio and TV talk show hosts just for the heck of it."

"Wow, I never knew," replied Candide.

"You bet," chuckled the man. "And that's a real fact too, unlike global warming."

When *Yeah!* paused for a commercial announcement, the audience leaped to its feet, cheering lustily and clapping madly. *It's good to be back in Freedonia,* thought Candide, as Chad shook his hand and the set technicians crowded around him, eager to thank their newfound savior.

That evening Chad and some of the senior network executives came by the bungalow to celebrate Candide's success with champagne and caviar. Everyone was eager to meet Miss Cunegonde, whom Candide had described as just an old-fashioned girl next door looking for the first available white picket fence. Chad was particularly taken with her, and, as the evening progressed, he adroitly maneuvered her into an unoccupied bedroom where they could have a cozy, private chat.

"I could get you on the show," said Chad, "but without a college degree and the usual references, you'll probably have to start off in the mailroom, perhaps while sleeping with me for the reality segment of the show."

"I don't know," replied Miss Cunegonde. "It sounds really complicated."

"We just call it reality TV, but it's not. You didn't know that?" said Chad, pressing himself tightly against the agreeably plush body of the young woman.

"Sure, I knew that. It's just that sometimes my brother gets pretty angry when it's becoming too hard for him to know what's real anymore," said Miss Cunegonde.

"Your brother's a great guy, and I'm sure he'd understand; but why bother him with real facts? Why not make every time a good time? Heck, that's why we always do the comedy segment right after the news," said Chad. He had positioned his hands inside Miss Cunegonde's blouse and was enjoying an expert squeeze of her breasts.

This particular tactic had always served him well in the past, and he would have certainly overcome Miss Cunegonde's various objections if the old woman had not come into the room at that moment, searching for a quiet spot to nap. Rather put out by this, Chad made his excuses and promptly left, giving the confused and somewhat aroused Miss Cunegonde the opportunity to inform her friend of what had just happened.

"You witless trollop," said the old woman. "What are you waiting for? He's powerful and wealthy, and, by the time he gets bored with you, you'll be sleeping with all of his rich friends anyway."

"Yeah, but he's kind of gross, too," sighed Miss

Cunegonde. "Hey, don't forget that my daddy was the CEO of Baron Incorporated, and my daddy always said that the best way to get rich was to never use your own assets—ever!"

"You're such a stupid slut that you wouldn't know what your assets were if they stood up and slapped you in your empty, kewpie doll face," snapped the old woman. "If I wasn't missing half of my internal organs, I'd sleep with this rich gringo pig right now for cab fare away from you and your brainless lover boy."

"Candide may be brainless, and he may not have as much money as Chad; but he probably looks much nicer naked, and sometimes being shallow like that is really more ethical for a girl like me, huh?" replied Miss Cunegonde.

And so on and so forth. The two women argued over the matter for quite a while, the youthful passion of the charming Miss Cunegonde pitting itself against the utter indifference of an ugly old woman. Such a frank discussion of the facts of modern romance might be useful for younger readers, but middle-aged readers will be relieved to hear that all of this was cut short by a loud howl of despair. Something was up in the front parlor of their bungalow.

The two women returned there to discover a group of network executives staring in horror at a TV screen, transfixed by a poorly-lit surveillance video of a man handcuffed to a chair. The man spoke slowly in a disjointed monotone, and, although he seemed to have fallen down several flights of stairs or possibly been run over by a car, his face was familiar.

"I'm a ... terrorist," mumbled Candide to the camera, "I'm a ... terrorist ... Freedonians ... just like you ... don't even know what's going on ... I'm a ... terrorist." The news crawl at the bottom of the screen summed things up nicely: Exclusive Video Confession of Sleeper Cell Terrorist Swearing Revenge on Freedonia!

"We're ruined! It's *Hell No!*—our competitors—the bastards!" moaned a network executive clutching his brow in despair. "We can't be seen negotiating with terrorists on air, no matter what their ratings are."

The mood in the bungalow turned ugly. Several of the executives broke up some of the furniture, and one of them slapped the Macarenan maid serving drinks. Chad wasted no time in telephoning security and telling them to hunt down Candide, but it was too late. Warned by the old woman, our young hero had already said goodbye to a tearful Miss Cunegonde and was climbing out of a bathroom window in the back of the bungalow.

"Man, this really sucks. I'm always going to be a screw-up," grunted Candide as he swung himself out of the narrow window and dropped onto the ground below. "Nothing I do ever comes out right. I'll never be a genuine, better than best Freedonian."

"Only a Freedonian is stupid enough to want to be a Freedonian," replied the old woman. "Shut up and run away! Being a stupid living Freedonian is a cupcake compared to being a stupid dead terrorist."

XIV
How Candide and Sanjay Busted Loose

CHAD'S PERSONAL ASSISTANT, SANJAY, WAS HAPPY to assist Candide out of the bathroom window and into Chad's expensive, fully loaded SUV. The sophisticated electronic anti-theft devices embedded in the machine were easily foiled by the bright young man, and, within seconds, they were driving away from the bungalow at top speed.

"I have already taken the precaution of hacking into Mr. Chad's bank account to provide us with sufficient funds for our escape," remarked Sanjay as he drove with one hand clutching his turban lest it unravel in the breeze.

"That's awesome, Sanjay. I'm really glad I met you while I was escaping," said Candide.

"Nothing that happens to us in this world is an accident, Mr. Candide," replied Sanjay. "I was fated to be plucked from a call center to be made into Mr. Chad's personal assistant. Mr. Chad was fated to shout at me all the time, mocking my accent, and ruining my marriage prospects. You were fated to be a terrorist instead of a cable TV celebrity. But as we can see, the great wheel of life has turned once again and left Mr. Chad thoroughly discomfited."

"I didn't trust that Chad guy either," agreed Candide. "I saw him making eyes at my girl. Who's the real terrorist now, huh?"

"Nonetheless, his limited sense of animal cunning may be of some use," said Sanjay. "Let us hoist him by his own lascivious petard. Do you remember how he thanked you for fighting the global warmers? I suggest that you now fight for the global warmers! Neither Mr. Chad nor the authorities will think of looking for you in the ranks of your former enemies."

"Excellent plan, Sanjay! No wonder you guys are so smart," said Candide. "I'd forgotten about being a so-called terrorist on the run. I guess I'm still a bit shook up by having to leave Miss Cunegonde so suddenly."

"I am certain you will meet her soon, in this life or your next," replied Sanjay cheerfully.

"But where are these global warmers? They must be pretty dangerous dudes."

"No doubt. I believe that they have entrenched themselves within the vast underground deposits of fossilized dollars that lie beneath the surface of Freedonia. They are converting this cash into greenhouse gases in illicit carbon trading markets which are surreptitiously price indexed to the specific gravity of the average Freedonian's wallet."

Candide was quite impressed by this. "I can't believe Chad made fun of your Freedonian accent. I mean, your communication skills are excellent. I don't even know what you just said, but I clearly understood every word."

"As a polytheist, I have to be careful. You never know who might be listening in," replied the young Hindu.

"Thank god Jesus was an only child, huh?" said Candide.

"Correct as always, Mr. Candide. These global warmers think much as you do. Despite the money it makes them, they abjure science as a transparent lie. To profit from a deeply held disbelief requires abundant spiritual backbone.

I have long wanted to meet these men and bask in their spiritual aura."

Candide agreed wholeheartedly to this. Although he yearned to return to Miss Cunegonde's plush embraces, he also yearned to stay well clear of any further trouble with the authorities. After driving for several days at top speed upon the spacious and well-designed Freedonian highways, they reached the hidden lair of the global warmers.

In the midst of a featureless plain stood thousands of oil-drilling derricks, all of them painted a bright, cheerful shade of green. The road weaved through this forest of derricks for several miles and then reached the crest of a low hill. A cinderblock wall trimmed with electrified concertina wire loomed before them. A video surveillance camera atop the heavy, blast-proof gate swiveled noisily to examine them more closely.

After a lengthy pause, the intercom squealed into life. "Anything to declare?"

"Just that Freedonia is the better than best place on earth," shouted Candide. The camera swiveled onto Sanjay.

"We're going to need documentation on this one," it said.

"We need to talk to whomever's in charge," replied Sanjay. "We just drove three thousand miles in an air-conditioned, fully-loaded SUV to help out global warming."

There was another lengthy pause. The gate swung open, and our heroes drove cautiously into the walled compound. It seemed deserted, only a few small, windowless blockhouses surrounding a concrete silo. They got out of their vehicle and waited for someone to appear.

"Where is everybody?" asked Candide. Sanjay shrugged his shoulders and scrutinized the reinforced steel door at the base of the silo. He cautiously pushed it open. The building was empty, except for the elevator whose doors soundlessly parted when the two men approached it.

"This is really creepy," whispered Candide.

"And uncomfortably cinematic, Mr. Candide," added Sanjay as he pressed the control panel's only button. The elevator doors closed, and they began to descend, plunging downwards at an ever-increasing velocity for what seemed a very long time.

The elevator came to an abrupt, perfectly cushioned halt. Its doors whisked open to reveal an enormous, reinforced concrete and steel dome sheltering a labyrinthine bunker of office cubicles. A few potted plants were the only signs of life in the dimly lit, soundless chamber.

The pale, blue light of a flickering computer monitor was seeping out of one of the cubicles. A man inside the cubicle was studying the monitor intently while smoking a cigarette. There was a heap of extinguished cigarette butts spilling out of the aluminum tray of his half-eaten TV dinner. His three-piece suit looked slept in, his tie was awry. The man glanced up at Candide and Sanjay. His seamy, patchwork face seemed to have been deflated and somehow ... re-inflated.

"Hey, Candide," grunted Junior Baron.

"Gee, is that you, Junior? You look, uh, flatter," replied the startled Candide.

"Impressive, three thousand miles in a fully-loaded SUV at top speed," replied Junior, "and just to help out with global warming. Who's the geek?"

"This is Sanjay. He figured out where you guys are hiding. I mean, you're one of the global warming guys, right?"

Junior's blue eyes narrowed.

"Even more impressive," he murmured. "Did Sanjay figure out that each one of those friendly, ecological-looking oil drilling derricks outside is actually pumping raw crude back into the earth?"

"Not yet, Junior," said Candide. "But guess what? The illegal alien home invasion guys didn't really kill your sister, Miss Cunegonde. She got away from them, and she's in Wollyhood right now."

Junior kept studying his monitor.

"Big deal. Being assaulted by illegal aliens is a cream puff compared to global warming. Global warming is the ultimate threat. It's the Just-Do-It®, Be-All-You-Can-Be®, Have-It-Your-Way® of our generation, and everything it touches turns to solid branding gold. Anyway, what the illegal alien dope fiends did to me was a lot worse than whatever they did to Miss Cunegonde."

Candide was rather nonplussed by these comments, but Sanjay managed to formulate his struggling thoughts for him.

"How did you survive being stomped to death by South American dope fiends?" asked Sanjay.

XV
How Candide Kicked Out the Jams

"EASY. I WENT FULL HALF-WIT ON THEM," SAID
Junior Baron. "They never saw it coming. I took
the ball right out of their hands and moved their
whole game to the next level, completely outside
their own box."

"Sweet," said Candide.

"Yeah, I know. I tuned out the screaming and
the blood and went really deep inside my own
head, into this weird mental mode where I was
so shallow that they couldn't stomp me any thinner. When the cops arrived, they rushed me to
a nearby hospital where a surgeon reinflated me
to a normal human pressure."

Junior's misaligned grimace was unsettling,
but he pressed on with his disturbing story.

"Now that dad's dead, I'm the CEO of Baron Incorporated. We're doing great things here, Candide. Last week a marlin fisherman in the Gulf of Mexico was mauled to death by an angry polar bear. That bear didn't swim all the way from the North Pole by accident. He was part of an international, animal flash mob that we can assemble in seconds, thanks to those endangered species radio collars we've hijacked.

"We call it Neo-Environmentalism. Baron Incorporated's lobbying subsidiary, Green Piece®, is handling the PR, and they've already come up with a media narrative: *working together to protect global warming from being endangered by government over-exploitation of natural resources.* Heck, it's no fair picking on carbon and oxygen. They're as natural as any other resource. In fact, we just rebranded all of the greenhouse gases as carbonated air. It's as safe as any other carbonated drink already on the market, and it won't make you fat either."

Junior resumed studying his computer screen. Candide scratched his head, overwhelmed by the unexpected enormity of their task. Even Sanjay seemed taken aback.

"You always did talk big, Junior Baron," said

Candide. "And like Doctor Pangloss said, those other guys may have their facts, but in the marketplace of facts, everything's equal. That's what makes science so democracy. Anyway, we're here to help you out for now. At least until Miss Cunegonde and I get married—probably as soon as everybody forgets about me being a terrorist."

Junior Baron spun around in his chair, his face livid with rage. "You want to marry my sister? After she just inherited fifty percent of the largest military-industrial multinational corporation in Freedonia? Look, Candide, I'm about to take global warming public with a six billion dollar IPO, and I'm not going to have it screwed up by some useless white trash loafer. You marry Miss Cunegonde? Over my dead body!"

If this chapter seems unusually brief and particularly sanguine to the reader, it is the fault of our literal-minded hero. On an earlier occasion, his sinewy but well-meaning heart had goaded him into killing both Señor and Colonel Armando with one pistol shot. This time, Candide's brain was responsible. Upon hearing the words "over my dead body," it flew into a whirlwind of mental activity which boded ill for the gabby Junior Baron. Within seconds a decision had been reached, and

Candide began kicking, punching, and pummeling the young businessman into a shapeless, deflated heap of a squashed, young businessman. The heady cocktail of literalism mixed with the hormonal excesses of young lust had hijacked our hero's moral compass with the usual, tragic results.

"Junior Baron's very words have furnished the seeds of his own destruction and final deflation," murmured Sanjay. "For him too, the wheel of life has turned distinctly sticky. Such are the mysterious dictates of karma. Hopefully, his next life will prove more personally congenial to him."

Candide's brain had not calmed down. He cut short Sanjay's eulogy with a sudden cry of alarm.

"Hey, we have to get out of here and we don't have much time. In a few minutes, every global warmer in this place will be after us."

The two young men fled Junior's cubicle and regained the elevator. By the time they had reached the surface and jumped into their SUV, the alarm had been raised. Strobe lights flashed, klaxons wailed, and loudspeakers barked orders to the armed men pouring out of the bunker—in vain. Candide and Sanjay had already sped off to safety.

XVI
In Which Candide and Sanjay Freak Out Some Freaks

If Candide could address the reader right now, he would probably apologize for both the breakneck pace and pixelated tenor of his adventures so far. Modern literature evolved beyond that sort of thing long ago, and an easy-to-swallow plot enlivened with a soupçon of ironic handwringing is all the rage today. The idea of a fictional hero running afoul of angry fathers, jihadi terrorists, secret police, corporate mercenaries, narco smugglers, a cable TV network, and a secret cabal of global warmers simply boggles the modern reader's mind, an authorial fate worse than death.

Yet Candide had little say over his fate, literary

or otherwise, for he lived in a world not of his own making. Like many Freedonians, he believed that he lived in a world of god's making, a chaotic and rather pointless mental arrangement. Over and over, Candide would flee the scene of one reversal for yet another, blissfully unaware of any method of dealing with life's complex problems other than relying on providence to furnish more of the same later on. Which was why Sanjay and he were now driving at top speed in their stolen SUV through the Freedonian heartland, determined to evade their latest pursuers.

Night had fallen, and they had left the underground lair of the global warmers far behind them. Their journey had been uneventful, at least until the collision of their SUV with an ornately dressed man pursuing a half-naked woman across an unlit city street. Taken by surprise, Candide swerved too late. The hapless man bounced off their vehicle in a flurry of gold chains and curses, and Candide accelerated to escape the chaotic scene.

"You jerks," shouted the woman, shaking her fist at them as they sped away. "You just killed my boyfriend."

Candide's eyes narrowed, something was

clearly amiss. "Probably an urban cult looking for teenaged runaways to prey on," he told Sanjay. "She'll thank me later when the drugs they gave her wear off."

"It is all very well to say *cherchez la femme* to impressionable young men," replied Sanjay, "but one must first teach them to look both ways before crossing the street."

"Yeah, huh? It's kind of like what's been happening to me. My life would be such a bummer if I didn't already know that somehow, someday, Miss Cunegonde and I would be back together."

"It is only logical, Mr. Candide," replied Sanjay. "God would not have made you kill her brother if he did not have something extra nice saved up for you later on."

"I guess all of god's children really do have to suffer before they can enjoy their just deserts," said Candide. "Isn't that something, running the human race like kids eating broccoli at the dinner table?"

The young man gazed through his tinted windows at the shabby wasteland of foreclosed and abandoned houses surrounding them, the infamous suburban underbelly of modern Freedonia. The scenery was an impressive testimony to the erosive powers of sun, wind, and money, but they had no time for sightseeing. It was getting late, and they needed to rest before continuing their journey. Candide brought their vehicle to a halt beneath a trash-strewn highway underpass and switched off the engine. Within moments, both men were asleep.

When they awoke, they were surprised to discover that they could not move. They were lying on the ground outside their vehicle, their hands and feet tightly bound together. Their captors glared at them.

"That's the asshole who killed my boyfriend," said the woman who had cursed them earlier. Both she and the other street people were clad in vaguely oriental rags. Their unwashed faces were transfixed by an impressive quantity of metallic pins, bolts, screws, and chains.

"You dudes are going to pay for this," said a young man unsteadily as he struggled to maintain his equilibrium despite himself.

"We have fallen into the clutches of some species of urban tribe, Mr. Candide," whispered Sanjay. "Do not be alarmed. My turban conceals a brain naturally endowed with a fiendish capacity for splitting the mental hairs of such Occidentals.

Our captors possess the collective mental capacity of a headless chicken and will be like putty in my hands."

"Dudes going to pay," mumbled the young man again, his attention clearly flagging.

"Yes, the cycle of life has finished with your late friend," announced Sanjay loudly. "Yet Mr. Candide and I, the agents of his karmic destiny, must remind you that his end was but a beginning. Which is why we must call him your late friend for he was clearly late for a new beginning. Fortunately, we arrived in time to begin his ending—although I must warn you that it is far too early for our own."

"Dude," said the young man.

"To end before you begin is the ultimate germination of one's karmic seeds. Please join with me in acknowledging your late friend's impending arrival into another, more congenial womb as both the birth of a nation and the death of a salesman."

"Wow. How did you know that T-Bone was a salesman in real life?" interrupted the young man.

"But what was he selling?" continued Sanjay. "The illusion of reality—or the reality of illusion?"

The young man was perplexed by this, but the young woman had an answer.

"I guess ... he was selling ... me," she said. "We were following the Dead, and we needed gas money. It was OK, actually. It's not like he owned me, you know?"

Candide was alarmed by this necrophiliac intimation, but Sanjay signaled him to remain silent.

"In that case you must release us to fulfill your own karmic destiny. We are on your side. You see, my companion has also just killed The Man!"

"Dude," said the mob in unison.

"Exactly. We need to get away as soon as possible before they find us," said Sanjay.

The street freaks released our heroes from their bonds and apologized to them for this inconvenience. With much backslapping and good cheer, they brought Candide and Sanjay to their urban lair, an abandoned shelter for derelicts where they arranged a hasty feast to celebrate the occasion. Later that evening, they led Candide and Sanjay to the edge of the city.

The young woman pointed toward the distant mountains. "This highway is the quickest route to the hidden paradise our Freedonian ancestors once spoke of. You'll be safe there from

The Man. It is called Kreationland. It's surrounded by impenetrable mountains, but your SUV can probably handle it."

"Thanks, freaks," said Candide. "Rock on."

"Yes, please keep it real," added Sanjay.

And they sped off in their vehicle.

XVII
In Which Candide and Sanjay
Discover That History is Bunk

"Perhaps we should return to Wollyhood," said Sanjay as he drove their SUV along the steep, curving mountain roads. "This quest for a hidden Freedonian paradise is inflaming my latent Occidentalism."

"That's got to hurt," replied our hero.

"You are correct as always, Mr. Candide. Occidentalism is the prejudiced fantasy of Freedonian life which many of my less enlightened countrymen entertain. It is a nightmare of blonde sex kittens, gun-wielding Christian mullahs, and shamelessly easy credit."

"If only, huh?" said Candide. "Anyway, Doctor Pangloss used to talk about Kreationland all the time, and, if he were alive, he'd want us to check it out."

Their journey through the mountains grew more difficult, and their powerful SUV labored to negotiate the winding roads that led them ever higher toward the legendary heartland of Freedonia. The air grew thinner, their ascent grew steeper, and the SUV's speed lessened until they were barely crawling forward. Just when the machine could ascend no farther, the road leveled off. They had reached a plateau surrounded by lofty, snow-capped peaks beneath the crystal-line dome of an azure sky interspersed with perfectly white, fluffy clouds. It looked suspiciously paradisiacal, and as they drove deeper into this concealed valley of verdant meadows, sparkling streams, and unspoiled forests, their suspicions were pleasantly confirmed.

Signs of human habitation appeared. Candide and Sanjay drove by endless miles of white picket fences and flocks of fresh-faced urchins eyeing the hot apple pies cooling on every windowsill. Tall, blonde-haired and blue-eyed gentleman farmers waved vigorously at Sanjay as he drove by their small but cozy plantation mansions.

These distractions were probably what led to

their next mishap. As Sanjay was accelerating to overtake a convoy of little red wagons, each one of them piloted by a chubby-cheeked, golden-curled toddler, a gigantic, bird-like creature swooped upon their SUV. It was a pterodactyl, and it was trying to carry off their vehicle with its massive talons.

The shaken Sanjay struggled with the steering wheel, battling to escape the angry dinosaur's clutches when a saber-toothed tiger leaped upon the hood of the SUV and began hammering at the windshield with its deadly fangs.

"Dude, do something," shouted Candide. The vehicle began to rock back and forth, its steel body crumpling and fracturing under the impact of the angry creatures' attack. Someone was shouting loudly in the distance.

"Hey, cut that out," barked a man wearing a three-cornered hat and bifocal spectacles. The startled beasts slunk off quietly while Candide and Sanjay stared at their rescuer's powdered wig, embroidered coat, and satin breeches.

"Those darn critters, they get spooked by strangers. They meant no harm though," said the man, extending a friendly hand toward Candide. "Welcome to Kreationland, folks. My name's Ben."

"I'm Candide," replied our hero, "and this is my personal assistant, Sanjay."

Ben stared at Sanjay. "That's quite some tan you got there," he said.

He turned to Candide. "You must have gone through a lot to get here so I'll show you around right away." He motioned them to follow him as he began walking toward the houses in the distance.

"We're doing better than best things at Kreationland," said Ben, "thanks to the amazing way that science keeps proving over and over that god's got his finger in every pie if we just face facts and start believing. Plus, there's no darn government red tape breathing down our necks."

He gestured at the meadow they were passing. A ragtag band of 18th-century New England cavemen were shooting their muskets at the redcoat-clad cavemen milling around the other end of the field. Ben beamed at the sight.

"These are our Lexington and Concord re-enactors. Pretty amazing, huh? Each one of them spends a small fortune on his costumes and weapons; it's not easy getting every detail perfectly authentic, but that's what we're aiming for in Kreationland."

A grinning Neanderthal in a British general's uniform waved at them as they passed by and the battle resumed. Several pterodactyls swooped overhead, strafing the cavemen with coconuts. One of the coconuts ricocheted into the next field, where a restive mob of black slaves with shiny new chains around their well-pedicured bare feet had gathered around a bearded, regal-looking white man in voluminous robes. He was lecturing them with the assistance of the oblong stone tablets he was using as flash cards. Although the bright sunlight made it difficult to see clearly, his leonine head seemed to be topped off with a shimmering golden halo.

"That's Moses," said Ben. "Don't worry, we switch off his halo when it rains. It's amazing, the way he can explain things to the field slaves. Sure, everyone wants to go down to the Promised Land, but why bother when things are just so much nicer on the plantation?"

Moses waved at Ben and resumed his lecture. "He'll set them straight soon enough, the rascals," Ben chuckled. "Did you know that most slaves in colonial times had better dental work and table manners than your average modern Freedonian? Heck, if that doesn't make you think twice about certain so-called historical facts, I don't know what will."

Sanjay cleared his throat. "Perhaps an arithmetical error is involved, but I cannot help noticing that those cowboys setting fire to the Egyptian pyramids are riding woolly mammoths instead of horses."

Ben's face darkened. "Son, there's no need to show off your college degree around here. All men are created equal in Kreationland, and this includes timelines and science and all that sort of stuff. Anyway, that's our Sons of Israel rodeo. It turns out that the Jews built the pyramids right before the dinosaurs went extinct, except that they weren't even Jewish to begin with. Most of them were Pentecostals, a few of them were Methodists. The main thing is that they could ride hard and shoot straight, just like Jesus would have if Pharaoh had let him."

"Man, this is awesome," interrupted Candide. "It's just like Doctor Pangloss told us. It's all starting to make sense now."

"Your Doctor Pangloss sounds like a pretty smart guy to me," said Ben as he led them past a collection of rough-hewn log cabins. In the front yard of each cabin, an army of worn-out women in bonnets and crinoline dresses was boiling water, chopping wood, and mending clothes for the immense swarm of noisy, barefoot children that crawled and leaped and scurried everywhere. A few men in coonskin caps relaxed in the warm sunshine, smoking their corncob pipes and smiling broadly while they whittled scraps of wood into birth control pills.

"We tried building enough one-room schoolhouses for all of the kids," admitted Ben, "but in the end it was simpler to let them run around barefoot all day, catching runaway slaves and whitewashing picket fences."

"Heck, just reading a newspaper nowadays is like taking your life into your own hands," added Candide.

Ben nodded his approval of this sentiment while leading the two travelers toward a small, well-kept park behind the log cabins, an oasis of tropical trees and flowers set beside a sparkling mountain stream. A herd of brontosauruses were placidly munching on the vegetation while Adam and Eve huddled around a potbellied stove, playing checkers atop a cracker barrel. A small war party of Plains Indians was lurking in the bushes behind them, horsing around with their smallpox-infected blankets despite strict instructions from the Archangel Michael not to do so.

"Kids do the darndest things, huh?" said a voice behind Candide. He turned around to find a man at his elbow, neatly dressed in a spotless white laboratory coat and brandishing a clipboard.

"Howdy, folks. I'm Gerry, the CEO of Kreationland," said the man.

XVIII
In Which White Makes Right

GERRY CHUCKLED AT CANDIDE'S AMAZED expression. "Oh, you mean this," he said, gesturing at his lab coat. "Don't worry, I'm not a scientist. I was just making fudge brownies in our research laboratory." Gerry slipped off the white coat, revealing himself to be dressed in the homespun loincloth and rawhide jerkin of a Palestinian shepherd, circa 30 AD. He replaced his clipboard with a shepherd's crook and offered a plate of freshly-baked brownies to the two travelers.

"The so-called noble savage is just an urban legend, as these Sioux warriors are demonstrating here," said Gerry. "But the Garden of Eden really did look like this to our original pioneer ancestors, Adam and Eve. In fact, this park is my favorite place in all of Kreationland. I wish more Freedonians could share this spiritual experience, but for now, we have to remain low-key. Manifest Destiny wasn't built in a day."

"These brownies are really good," said Candide.

"Yes, they are," agreed Sanjay. "But I am curious, how did you stay so well hidden for so long?"

"Hey, why do you think I'm dressed as a Palestinian shepherd in the time of Jesus? We're totally off the grid!" said Gerry. Ben nodded at this, his powdered wig and three-cornered hat bobbing up and down.

Sanjay persisted. "If this is the real Freedonia, why doesn't Freedonia look like this?"

"Appearances don't need facts to account for them," replied Gerry, "and facts certainly don't require appearances. Heck, doesn't what I just said appear a lot like a fact itself, when you think about it?"

"Why are there dinosaurs in your Bible? Is that a typo?" asked Sanjay, by now rather put out by the threadbare tenor of monotheism. Polytheism seemed far more—what was the word?—stereophonic to him.

"Look, all of the animals in the Bible were an important food source for the cavemen, not just dinosaurs," explained Ben. "If god had not meant them to be eaten, why did he make them out of meat? Hamburger sure doesn't grow on trees. And by the way, our god doesn't play with his food, unlike some other so-called religions we know."

Ben and Gerry stared pointedly at the turbaned Sanjay. An uneasy silence weighed upon the scene until someone standing behind them discreetly cleared his throat.

"Gentlemen, lunch is being served in the D.W. Griffith Tea Room," announced a smartly liveried butler who bore a startling resemblance to the Piltdown Man.

"Thank you, Benson," replied Gerry. "We'll be right there. Candide must be hungry and thirsty after his long journey."

Our two heroes, their hosts, and an assortment of biblical prophets, antebellum cotton planters, Kentucky backwoodsmen, and Neolithic cavemen gathered to eat in a spacious dining room modeled upon the luncheon counter of a southern Woolworth's in the 1950s. The food was plentiful, and both Candide and Sanjay ate well.

"Man, I can't believe how good everything tasted in the past," said Candide.

"What's really amazing is that this is also the future," replied Gerry. "In a few years, all of Freedonia will look like this if we remain strong and pure like the Founding Fathers intended us to. Meanwhile, both of you are welcome to relax in our forbidden, lost paradise for as long as you like. Even you, Sanjay. Just put a baseball cap over that turban, find yourself a mop and a bucket, and stay out of trouble, OK?"

Both Candide and the reader will be pleased to learn that this point in our narrative marks an intermission, a well-deserved holiday from the whirlwind, hectic pace of our story so far. Three square meals, clean sheets, and easy living would now be the order of the day for our hero.

Candide worked hard on his golf game with Ben and Gerry, who were avid duffers themselves. They also owned a bass-fishing boat, and Candide had an open invitation to join them whenever he liked. On rainy days it was lunch at the clubhouse, where a bevy of stylishly uniformed young waitresses waited upon them with Nordic efficiency. After lunch, Candide napped on the sofa of his air-conditioned executive suite until the Scandinavian masseuse arrived, a demure but attractive girl who came personally recommended by his new friends. It was all strictly above board, of course. The legions of vaguely Germanic female domestics who fed, clothed, and cleaned up after the men of Kreationland wouldn't have it any other way—or so it seemed to our young hero.

One evening, Candide returned home with a platinum blonde housemaid who had attached herself to him at an ice cream social. It was getting late when they returned to his suite, and, as soon as they arrived, the young lady dimmed the lights, removed her go-go boots, and hopped onto the sofa.

"You're so good, you're the best. You're … the master," she said.

"Excuse me?" said Candide.

"You're so … in charge," she said.

"Thanks," said Candide, fending off the girl's limp embraces, "but I'm already engaged to Miss Cunegonde."

"That's OK. I only want to be … remembered … afterwards," she continued.

"Hey, what's on TV tonight?" asked Candide.

"Sure, I can watch if you want me to. I like to watch."

The exasperated Candide pushed her away forcefully, and the girl slid off the sofa, banging her head against the coffee table so sharply that it popped off her shoulders.

"Huh?" exclaimed Candide. The multicolored wires jutting from the base of the girl's severed head had become entangled with the legs of the coffee table. Her mouth worked spasmodically.

"Let me freshen you up ... freshen you up ... freshen you up."

A shadow moved through the darkness behind Candide, and the room's lights came on.

"Blonde but deadly, Mr. Candide," announced Sanjay. He picked up the severed head and pushed aside its beehive hairdo to examine its smoldering circuitry more closely. "As I suspected, one of Baron Incorporated's animatronic Help-Mates®," he said, "originally designed to channel international terrorism into repetitive sexual intercourse but now dragooned into cleaning up after Kreationland's burgeoning male population."

"Like a cheap horror movie," said Candide.

"Cheap but legal in most of the world's major religions, Mr. Candide. The allure of submissive young women is truly ecumenical. In any case, I've taken the liberty of hacking into Ben and

Gerry's database of stolen credit cards and transferring their ill-gotten gains directly into your bank account. And Mr. Chad's SUV has been repaired and is now parked outside your door."

"Good thinking, Sanjay. This was just a fake hidden paradise anyway. Let's go find Miss Cunegonde," said Candide.

He followed Sanjay outside into the cool night air. All of Kreationland was still asleep, but, once its inhabitants awoke and discovered that their secret had been exposed, our heroes' lives would be in grave danger. No Bible, no matter how elastic, could withstand this sort of revelation. Both men hopped into their vehicle and roared off at top speed.

By dawn, they had left the mountain redoubt of Kreationland far behind them and were driving toward New Shazizzle, the economic and cultural capital of Freedonia. It was rumored that if you could make it in New Shazizzle, you could make it anywhere, and, needless to say, our heroes were on the make.

XIX
In Which Candide Does Some Urban Multi-Tasking

"SO MUCH FOR THE FREEDONIAN DREAM," SIGHED Candide. "By the way, Sanjay, where were you all the time?"

"I must apologize for my absence," replied Sanjay, "but I was busy scrubbing dishes, trimming boxwood hedges, and keeping the washrooms tidy. After all that, hacking into the Kreationland database was child's play."

"Sweet. You had it all figured out. Those guys were total fakes."

"Yes, but by electronically diverting their finances, we have divested them of an onerous karmic burden. Eventually, they will understand the spiritual necessity of this."

"Ditto, I guess. Anyway, I want you to fly to Wollyhood and find Miss Cunegonde. If anybody makes problems, just use lots of money. And don't forget the old woman, or whatever's left of her."

"An excellent idea," replied Sanjay. "We can meet in the People's Republic of Wonton, the most populous nation on earth. We will evade our various pursuers by blending effortlessly into a sea of Wontonese."

As soon as they arrived in New Shazizzle, Candide drove his personal assistant to the airport. Sanjay would leave immediately for Wollyhood while Candide remained behind to tie up some loose ends. There was much to do, and Candide was determined to do it right. He was on a mission of love and damn the expense.

Within twenty-four hours he had paid a thousand dollars for a hotel room whose locks were the wrong size for its keys, a thousand dollars to the desk clerk who promised to look the other way while Candide slept in a coat closet, and another thousand dollars to the bellhop who promised not to report all of them to the management.

The next day Candide took a cab to the Wontonese embassy and was stopped for speeding by a roving insurance company agent. Since

Candide was the employer of the driver—technically speaking—the thousand-dollar fine came entirely out of his own pocket. The incident left him so shaken that he completed his journey on the subway, where he lost another thousand dollars on a game of chance with a fast-talking ten-year-old. When he returned to his coat closet that evening, he discovered that his thousand-dollar Wontonese entry visa had melted in the rain.

The next day, Candide collared the first pedestrian he met on the street. He was mad as hell, and he wasn't going to take it any more.

"This town is full of crooks," announced Candide to the startled man.

"What's it to you?" replied the man. "It's called full employment, you moron. Get away from me."

Another man pushing a rack of dresses down the sidewalk elbowed Candide out of his way. "That's right, dummy. This way, everybody knows where they are. The crooks, that is."

A large woman in a mumu jostled Candide aside. "Hey, you're always in the way. From out of town, aren't you?"

"I'm a visitor from small-town Freedonia," said Candide, "and I have to tell you that I think it stinks here."

A hairy man in a sweat suit jabbed his finger at Candide, shouting so vehemently that droplets of his spittle flew into Candide's eyes.

"Hey, asshole, beauty is in the eye of the beholder. Underneath all this rude indifference, New Shazizzle is just like any other small town in Freedonia. But because we're so big, our rude indifference just looks bigger. Jesus, are you thick or something?"

Several other pedestrians loudly cursed our young hero, and one of them ran off to fetch a policeman. Several hours later, Candide emerged from the local magistrate's office a thousand dollars poorer but infinitely wiser in the perils of accosting a pedestrian without probable cause on the streets of New Shazizzle.

From then on, Candide kept to his coat closet. He had booked a first-class seat on the next flight to Wonton, and to while away the time, he placed a notice in an internet chat room, offering to pay the travel expenses of anyone willing to accompany him on the trip. The successful applicant would have to be a genuinely honest—and thus a genuinely wretched—Freedonian. Candide had begun to be troubled by vague philosophical doubts about life in general and his own in particular—a philosophically-inclined traveling companion might be just the ticket for this angst-ridden young man.

Several dozen men turned up in the hotel lobby, all of them loudly cursing the government or pretending to find lost wallets, most of them reeking of strong drink and urine. Reminding himself of Doctor Pangloss' dictum to celebrate the differences that unite us by keeping oneself at a safe distance from the truly different, Candide remained in his coat closet. He busied himself with weeding out the more colorful candidates' applications and then began sifting through the few remaining resumés, searching for persons with a long history of persistent impoverishment.

One resumé in particular caught his eye. Merle was a poet, a once-noble calling which was now utterly beyond modern society's notice, much less its contempt. Merle had been robbed by his cheating wife, beaten up by his drug-addled son, and abandoned by his scatterbrained daughter. Even his dog had debunked long ago for greener pastures. He spent his days in the public libraries and parks to save on rent money, and he would have spent his nights in the nearest saloon, silently shedding a tear or two into his beer, but he did not go in for that sort of thing.

"I've never met a poet before," announced Candide to the startled man. "Anybody who makes as little money as you do has to be honest. Pack your bags, we're leaving tomorrow morning."

"Well, isn't that something," said Merle. And it certainly was.

XX
In Which Merle Ruminates Aloud

IT WAS A LONG FLIGHT TO WONTON, AND SINCE both the young man and the poet had seen a good deal of the world, they had much to talk about. Candide provided his new friend with a quick précis of his adventures so far.

"Life is tough, that's for sure," he concluded, "but at least I have Miss Cunegonde to look forward to."

"Once I gave up hope, I felt much better," replied Merle. "I advise you to do the same. Lowered expectations are the bread and butter of the lower classes. And don't talk to me about great expectations—read the book, saw the movie, and I'm not buying any of it."

"Merle, you have such a cool way of expressing

yourself. Was that one of your poems?" asked Candide.

"Yeah, probably," said Merle. "I compose true-life poetry instead of just getting on with my life, mostly because my life is scientific proof of the futility of trying to live it. Frankly, I blame the management, if you know what I mean."

"Wow, you're an atheist?" asked Candide. "Is that even legal?"

"Probably not. But I'm tired of playing hide-and-go-seek with someone who keeps bending the rules whenever things get too hot for him. I got news for god—two can play that game."

"Merle, you're a trip," said Candide. "I've never heard anybody talk like you in my entire life, not even Miss Cunegonde's old lady friend."

"That old lady friend of hers had the right idea. Survive, man, survive. Funkistani terrorists, Costaguanan narcos, secret torture chambers, they're all swimming pool piss-parties compared to just staying alive."

Candide glanced out of the window at the ocean beneath them. They were flying over a large, well-appointed yacht that had burst into flames. A flotilla of high-powered speedboats crammed with well-armed men swarmed around the stricken craft. The crew and passengers of the yacht waved frantically at the passing aircraft.

"Ladies and gentlemen," announced the pilot on the intercom, "there's no need for alarm, but, if you look toward the aircraft's port side, you might catch a glimpse of what appears to be a pirate attack upon a luxury yacht."

Candide peered through the smoke and flames at the well-dressed men and bikini-clad women in high heels trying to escape the motley swarm of pirates chasing after them.

He plucked at Merle's sleeve. "Hey, it's the little boy who ripped me off in the subway. The pirates are tying him up and dragging him and the others into their speedboats."

"There goes your thousand dollars," said Merle.

"I guess, huh? Doctor Pangloss was right. Justice will prevail, and things will always work out somehow for Freedonians, the better than best people on earth. I bet those pirates are going to teach that brat a lesson he'll never forget. Why doesn't he just ask his rich parents for pocket money instead of scamming strangers on the subway?"

"Probably some kind of character-building fad," said Merle, "but give him time, and he'll be scamming his own parents. Hustling lost tourists is just a way station on the subway of sin."

"Merle, that's your best poem yet. I can't believe you're not rich and famous from writing such great poetry."

Merle stared out of the window at the beleaguered yacht for a long time, his brow furrowed. He sighed loudly. "I have a confession to make," he said at last. "I'm not who you think I am."

XXI

In Which the Great White Hope Isn't

"I'M GOING TO LEVEL WITH YOU," SAID MERLE. "I'm not a poet at all, I'm an actor. All of this is preparation for my next motion picture role as an urban, street-wise poet who lives in an underground loft and battles the zombie menace of a dead poets' society."

Candide did not know what to say to this.

"Yeah, I know," continued Merle, "it's probably direct-to-pirated-video in the Third World, but my agent says even that would be a real step up for me."

"Merle, I hired you because I thought you were honest, but this doesn't sound very honest to me," said Candide.

"Maybe not honest *per se* but perhaps painfully honest, which is even better, physically speaking. Hey, treasure it, man, and just go with the flow for now. And by the way, my real name's Wadsworth."

Candide watched in amazement as his companion tugged at his face, working free the white, molded-latex mask concealing his genuine black features.

"You try finding work as an action hero, even in blank verse, when you're black," said Wadsworth. "I thought that going whiteface would help out, but let me tell you, it was a real hassle, especially with the ladies."

"What about the abusive family and your dog running away?" asked Candide.

"I'm the unmarried son of loving, middle-class parents who furnished me with an excellent education. But my dog did run away after I put on the whiteface."

Candide scratched his head. What would Doctor Pangloss have done in such a situation?

"So what you're really saying is that this is not me and whatever I say is just a lie," said our hero.

"I just want to finish this picture and get paid," replied Wadsworth. "Deception and reality are pretty much the same, Candide, otherwise it wouldn't really be deception, would it? You'd always spot it before it had time to do its deception thing and then what would you be left with? Just another sordid reality. And who's going to pay ten bucks to see that?"

Their airplane began to descend toward the jungle stretching toward the horizon in every direction. They had reached the halfway point of their journey, the Democratic Republic of Savoy, where they would land and await the next connecting flight to Wonton. Candide had reserved a luxury suite in a hotel, and as their taxi took them there, he and Wadsworth continued their conversation.

"Do you really believe in atheism?" asked Candide.

"Sure, why not?" replied Wadsworth. "You have to believe in something, and atheism is better than nothing. It's tough love, and that's probably what god needs right now."

The taxi driver, an elderly Savoyard, was flummoxed by his passengers' moral turpitude. "What foolishness you Freedonians are talking. If there's no god, then who made the world?"

"Who made your taxi cab?" asked Wadsworth.

"Do you need to know every time you start the motor? Anyway, the vehicle comes with an AM/ FM radio, so just buckle up, man, and enjoy the ride."

The taxi driver shook his head at this but brightened up when Wadsworth tipped him at the hotel. "Perhaps atheists tip better," he admitted, "but this is because they do not know that they should be saving their money for the next world. Taxis are not cheap there either, gentlemen."

Without waiting for a reply, the man drove off before his vehicle's tires were stolen again.

XXII
How Candide Was
Rumbled in the Jungle

THE AFRICAN NATION OF SAVOY WAS, AS THE hotel's brochure noted, a vibrant and exciting land of an unrelenting tropical exuberance. Candide immediately contracted amoebic dysentery and fled into the washroom. Wadsworth sent for a doctor although the desk clerk sent a prostitute to their room instead. When Candide returned from the washroom, the woman gave him some antibiotic pills she had in her voluminous purse.

"Are you homosexuals?" she asked the two men. "Because I can cure that also."

"No, but thanks anyway. Our health care system in Freedonia is pretty good," replied Candide, rather weakly.

"My bunga-bunga system is much better," giggled the woman.

The muffled sound of a distant explosion rocked the building, and the woman left in a hurry. Wadsworth tried to turn on the color television to see what was up, but the set had vanished. The clock radio was also gone, as were their watches, jewelry, and petty cash. Another explosion rocked the building. Wadsworth pushed aside the drapes and peered outside. In the distance, people were shouting as they broke windows and set tires alight.

Wadsworth shook his head. "Looks like a lot of the rioters are disguising themselves as policemen … or maybe vice versa. Either way, it's a law enforcement nightmare out there."

They took the elevator down to the lobby, but all of the hotel staff had fled except for the desk clerk. "There is no problem at all," he announced. "Please be happy, all foreigners, and enjoy your stay in the Democratic Republic of Savoy during this festive season of national elections."

A white man in a safari suit approached them. He was sweating profusely and spoke so rapidly that Candide and Wadsworth had difficulty understanding him.

"I'm Abbott," he said. "I'm a fellow Freedonian just like you. Perhaps we could join forces, pool our resources, make common cause, you know, whatever it takes, huh?"

A machine gun began firing nearby. Abbott wiped his sweat-drenched forehead with a limp sheet of newspaper.

"Oh, you noticed?" he said before they could reply. "That's right, I'm a journalist. I'm with the Homey Shopping Network. We work with African dictators, despots, strong men, whatever you call them. We have a solid lock on the suburban white gangsta-wanna-be demographic."

"Sounds like box office gold," said Wadsworth. "I have a dream, you have a dream, eyes on the prize behind door number three, yeah, I get it."

"And nobody works harder for that dream than an African despot," said Abbott. "It's rags-to-riches plus hot chicks plus Freedonian military aid equals tropical hip-hop paradise."

"Why's everyone so upset?" asked Candide. "Rampaging Savoyard mobs demanding more democracy for their democracy-ravaged nation, it doesn't make sense."

Abbott flinched as an automobile exploded

across the street. "It's mostly disgruntled high school math teachers protesting President Foufou's re-election by a substantial, though technically negative number of votes."

"It figures, huh? High school teachers are always turning elections into cheap popularity contests," said Candide.

"There's a lot of conspiracy theories going around," said Abbott. "Those Get-Out-The-Voter® electronic polling booths from Baron Incorporated killed a lot of barefoot citizens. Who knew that electronic voting in this humidity was so dangerous?"

"I just remembered something," said Wadsworth. "Savoy has the largest bling deposits in the world. President Foufou is the only man standing between those resources and international terrorists trying to build a dirty bling bomb."

"Sweet," said Candide.

The next day Candide woke up feeling much better. Abbott had moved in with them during the night, emptying the mini-bar and making a pig's sty of the washroom. The color television had reappeared, as had the Savoyard prostitute, who was giving Wadsworth a full-body massage. The air conditioning had broken down, and the room reeked of marijuana, baby oil, and cheap scent.

"Hey, Candide, chill out. Everything's OK now," said Wadsworth.

"You Freedonians are so tense," purred the woman. "You must learn to relax like the IMF soldiers, tiger."

President Foufou was addressing the nation on the television. "In a world of senseless violence, politics should be fun," he said peevishly. "I am a funny guy. I have a sense of humor. All Savoyards will laugh with me now."

Abbott was playing cards with another Savoyard sitting on a crate of iced beer, a man who introduced himself to Candide as the prostitute's brother, Sid.

"Oh, Candide," said Abbott, "someone calling herself Miss Cunegonde left a message for you while you were asleep. She's waiting for you in an abandoned house near the airport. Sid can drive us there."

The prostitute's brother smiled at Candide. "Such good news, Mr. Candide," he said. "We will all go together. Mr. Abbott, my sister and I will make sure that Miss Cunegonde and you have a warm Savoyard welcome."

The jet-lagged Wadsworth stayed behind to take a nap. When he awoke several hours later, Candide had returned. He was alone, and he seemed unusually subdued.

"How did it go?" asked Wadsworth.

"It was too dark to see anything," said Candide, " but I think Miss Cunegonde asked me for five hundred dollars just to have sex with her. And Abbott is a pervert. He tried to watch until Sid threw him out. They made such a racket that the police fined me another five hundred dollars. Love sure stinks sometimes."

"It was all fake," said Wadsworth. "You are one lucky Caucasian, man, although that could have been one righteous, night of the iguana, urban jungle guerilla love-in, if that's your bag."

"I guess it is now," sighed Candide.

They caught the next airplane out of Savoy. On their way to the airport, Radio Savoy interrupted its normal programming for a special announcement. The taxi driver turned up the volume on his radio. Freedonian Special Forces troops had landed in the country and successfully taken control of the nation's strategic bling reserves. Bling futures on the stock market were trading at record highs, and white suburban

gangsta-wannabe shareholders felt what amount-
ed to a personal transformation. The Savoyard
spirit of excellence in bling production had been
reignited by the passion and inspiration of armed
Freedonians. And there was more good news.

"Rioting mathematics teachers have returned
to their classrooms," announced the radio, "after
assurances from President Foufou that he will
investigate their demands that the government
reinstate the numbers zero through one hundred
throughout most of the nation."

"Who needs such numbers anyway? They are
a rich man's luxury," shrugged the cab driver.
They reached the airport without further incident. Within an hour their jet had taken off, lazily
orbited this city of broken dreams and burning
tires and then begun to climb toward the east.

XXIII
In Which Candide and Wadsworth ♥ Darkness

CANDIDE LISTLESSLY PICKED AT HIS RECONSTITUTED filet mignon and tetra-packed red wine. They had been flying over Africa for several hours, and he had not spoken a word.

"Everybody's a jerk and a liar," he said at last. "Everywhere I go—Freedonia, Funkistan, Costa-guana, Savoy—it's always the same."

Wadsworth nodded. "Cheap air travel is the icing on the global village idiots' cake. The whole planet's screwed. There's no escape anymore."

"I feel like I'm a pawn in a sick, twisted game. Each one of my adventures is even dumber than the one before. It's like I'm plumbing the depths of moron, and it's never going to bottom out."

"Life's futile, man, but maybe it's better like that. There's nothing worse than a moron who believes in what he's doing because another moron gave him hope. I can't be that hope-moron for you, not yet, at least. Hey, look at that."

Wadsworth gestured at the window. A Freedonian battleship was anchored off the African coast beneath them. In the empty immensity of earth, sky, and water, she was firing into a continent. Her ensign dropped limp like a rag, the sea swell swung her up lazily and let her down. Her guns fired, a small flame darted out and vanished, a little puff of white smoke would appear.

"Damn, look at all that firepower," murmured Wadsworth. "It's too much, man, too much … the horror … the horror."

"Probably Savoyard math teachers making trouble again," sighed Candide.

A Freedonian serviceman on leave was sitting behind them. "Heck, no," he said. "Looks like we're bombarding another family planning clinic. Don't worry, we're probably shelling the area with pornographic videos and magazines, sex toys, whatever it takes to get these villagers to forget about the planning and get on with the family."

"Destroy them to save them, right?" said Wadsworth.

"Oh, nothing like that," chuckled the service-man. "It's mostly for the encouragement of mothers. You don't have anything against mothers, do you?"

Their airplane banked toward the east, and the warship vanished into the sea haze. There was nothing more to say. It was all very mysterious; a barrage of pornographic videos hurtling into the jungle, a young man flying overhead in a pressurized aluminum tube, an urbane black thespian haunted by white-faced nightmares—what did it all mean? Where were they going? Why were they there?

Such existential questions had vexed the finest minds of Freedonia for many years until these minds had come up with a startlingly effective solution, a saucy sort of explanation which was universally judged to be better than best once certain lesser-minded Freedonians had gotten over it.

"We're here because we're here," declared a Freedonian military chaplain to the shell-shocked soldiers shoveling the remains of their slaughtered comrades into body bags.

"History is bunk," announced a Freedonian

caveman to the dumbfounded, bloodied survivors of a renegade dinosaur attack.

"Just sell the sizzle," proclaimed an obese Freedonian tourist to the skeletal Third World child-beggars crowding around him, feebly clamoring for spare change.

Indeed, it is a scientifically proven fact that Freedonian life is more meaningful than most other lives, in particular those nasty, brutish, and short lives with unpronounceable foreign names. A Freedonian's life is sumptuously furnished with a mind-boggling supply of contradictory reasons to keep on living, even if nothing else he does has ever required a reason. The unexamined life of an ancient Greek philosopher might not be worth living, but the unexamined Freedonian life is a fully capitalized and going concern with definite prospects for advancement in a perpetually deferred afterlife.

Candide's thoughts on this very subject were percolating through his brain at that very moment, and they were not particularly flattering to Candide nor his maker.

Man, right now my life really sucks, but everything is going to be great from now on. I'm going to really miss being myself once I'm dead, he thought.

Wadsworth was thinking along the same lines but with considerably more urban panache.

The first thing I'm going to do when I die, he thought, *is move on up. Yes, sir!*

Both men fell asleep. When they awoke, the air hostess was making an announcement on the cabin intercom. "Ladies and gentlemen, we are preparing to land in Wonton. Please fasten your seat belts and adjust your trays to the upright and locked position."

Never before had Candide heard these words of federally-mandated, aviation safety precautions with such attentive delight. At last he had reached the financial and military heart of Asia, the Communist People's Republic of Wonton, where his beloved Miss Cunegonde and faithful personal assistant Sanjay awaited him.

I have to find you, Miss Cunegonde, murmured the young man to himself, *because life without you is meaningless, and that's a fact.*

XXIV
How Candide and Wadsworth
Learned That It Is What It Is

CANDIDE AND WADSWORTH SPENT A WEEK searching every hotel and bungalow and warehouse trailer in Wonton without finding any trace of either Miss Cunegonde or Sanjay. It became clear to Candide that Miss Cunegonde was probably dead for she couldn't possibly have forgotten about him so quickly. He spent a few nights weeping into his pillow.

"You're right," he announced to Wadsworth. "Life sucks. Everybody's miserable. What's the use of living?"

Wadsworth remained unperturbed. "That's cool. I've been the trash-talking, black sidekick in far too many cop buddy films not to know that whatever you say, that's the script as read."

"If there's a script to this, I feel sorry for the author," said the earnest young man.

Prescience is a queer thing, almost as queer as the convoluted Freedonian prejudices of this narrative. After taking a bash at the cultural foibles of Latin America, the Middle East, and Africa, it's only fair that we now take a swipe at the eccentricities of Asian society. More evolved readers can flaunt their *savoir faire* by triangulating all this Third World vilification with the many insults and insinuations that have already been heaped upon the people of Freedonia. Less evolved readers will have to make do with a snappy bromide, something along the lines of remembering that two or three or even four wrongs often do make a right, or at least muddy up each other's tracks so thoroughly that it amounts to the same outcome in the grand scheme of things.

None of this mattered much to Candide and Wadsworth. They were blissfully unaware of even being unaware, which explains why they were eating lunch in an open-air café when they heard some shocking news: a thousand Wontonese children would have been mortally poisoned by tainted milk-powder if an earthquake had not first brought their shoddily built schools down upon their heads.

"These Wontonese think they can get away with anything," said Candide, "but cutting corners will only get you so far. That's what's so cool about capitalism—even for communists."

Wadsworth fished some flotsam out of his bubble tea and flicked it onto the street. A mongrel sniffed it and went into convulsions. In six weeks, this serendipitous new dog repellent would permeate every lawn and living room sofa in Freedonia.

"They say that man is a bad animal," replied Wadsworth, "which is a step up for some of us when you look at the bigger picture."

Wadsworth signaled to the manager of the café to complain about the appalling hygiene of his establishment, but the man ignored him. He was weeping loudly and cursing the government, his child had been trapped in one of the doomed schools. A policeman spotted the distraught father and arrested him for public loitering. Several plainclothesmen who were also loitering nearby arrived in time to begin giving the malcontent the sound thrashing he so richly deserved.

"That's right, beat me," howled the man as

they kicked and punched him. "Beat me all you like. I'm a human being, not a beast like you." A police dog leaped upon him and finished him off. Our two travelers paid their bill and made a hasty exit.

Candide was puzzled. "Everybody makes somebody else out to be an animal. It's got to be upsetting for the real animals in the wild kingdom. They don't even have the brains to think up so many sadistic tortures."

"It's the System, man," said Wadsworth. "Sadism's become a family value just like all the others. If you don't believe me, just remember what god did to his only son."

"This could never happen in Freedonia," said Candide. "Jesus being killed, I mean."

They kept walking until they reached the edge of the city. It was a pleasant, green place of small gardens and tidy homes being crushed into rubble by an army of bulldozers. Those inhabitants who had survived their forced eviction gathered around a senior real estate developer. He had an announcement for them.

"The maladjusted *feng shui* of your homes will be rectified by luxury high-rises," he said, "where rich, childless couples can pamper the fortunate children whom the police removed from your un-sanitary hovels at great expense to these wealthy philanthropists."

"Man, it's like the zen of evil around here," said Wadsworth.

"I don't know. There has to be some kind of silver lining to all this," mused Candide. "Hey, look at those guys, they seem happy."

Candide pointed at the smiling young men streaming into a nightclub that had just opened its doors for the evening. The two travelers decided to see for themselves if this establishment harbored a happier, better-adjusted sort of Wontonese. After giving the doorman a hefty tip, they were whisked inside and escorted to their table by another handsome youth. The nightclub was crowded with well-dressed young men smoking cigarettes, drinking cocktails, and chatting gaily to one another. Two men wearing sequined tuxedoes were singing a karaoke duet on a raised stage, and, when they finished, their cheering Wontonese audience pelted them with a flurry of loose change.

One of the singers spotted Candide sitting at a table with Wadsworth and asked if he might join them. Candide gladly agreed and ordered a fresh round of drinks for everyone.

"My dear Candide," said the handsome, young man as he sipped his margarita, "don't you remember me? I'm Paco, the pool boy."

"Wow, I never would have guessed it was you underneath all that make-up," said Candide.

"It's part of my act," replied Paco. "And I'm sorry about giving AIDS to your friend Doctor Pangloss."

"That's OK. He survived long enough to be tortured to death afterwards."

"Ouch. Anyway, I got better after I crowd-funded the money for my antiviral treatment on the internet. It was mostly webcam work until I became the victim of a hostile take-over by a Wontonese syndicate. They human-trafficked me to an offshore sexual call center until a consultant from Baron Incorporated suggested that all content providers be replaced by looped soundtracks from public domain sex videos."

"Walmartizing the world's oldest profession in the digital age," chuckled Wadsworth, "you know that's going to get ugly real fast."

"I'm living *la vida loca,* guys," said Paco. "For years I was stuck at the Latino bottom of the Freedonian food chain, but I pass for WASP here. All the round-eyes look the same to the Wontonese."

"It sounds great if that's what makes you happy," said Wadsworth.

"Well, I'm gay, but I'm not happy-happy, if that's what you mean," replied Paco. "Although, I've felt a lot better since I found Jesus."

"That's awesome," said Candide.

Paco beckoned his singing partner to join them at their table. "This is Jesus," said Paco. "Thanks to him, I'm a lot happier. Jesus saved me."

"Paco's my number one fan," said Jesus, rolling his eyes theatrically. "He tells everybody that I've redeemed him, but, actually, I just help out with the rent and groceries."

"At least your audience appreciates you," said Candide. "That was quite a standing ovation they gave you after your performance."

"The Wontonese weren't applauding us," laughed Jesus. "They were mocking our Western decadence. They invented gunpowder, paper money, and the fortune cookie, but being gay never once crossed their minds."

"It's like they have some kind of mental block," said Candide.

"Probably," replied Paco. "Could you loan us twenty dollars for cab fare? I lost my wallet."

"He's always losing everything," sniffed Jesus. "Christ, give me a break."

Candide gave Paco and Jesus twenty dollars. Despite his misgivings concerning the human race, he was still proud to be a Freedonian, and, whether he's in a Wontonese gay bar or a Savoyard crime lair or even a Freedonian voting booth, a genuine Freedonian just can't help being better than best at being bested.

All four men left the nightclub and were standing on the sidewalk, enjoying the fresh evening air when Candide had another idea. *To heck with it,* he thought, *I'll give them both another twenty.*

And so he did. A moment later, a large, white limousine came to an abrupt halt in front of them. A pink-faced, stoutly built European man thrust his head out of the passenger's window and stared at Candide.

"By Jove, it's a *pukka* Freedonian!" declared the elderly gentleman. "I knew it as soon as I saw you lavishing such magnificent largesse upon two complete strangers."

He gestured at Candide and Wadsworth to

approach him. "I am Sir Crampton Hodnet, cultural attaché for Her Majesty's Government at the Vulgarian consulate. I would like both of you to join me for the evening. Drinks and small talk, culture, books, that sort of thing."

"Go riding in an air-conditioned limo with a real descendant of Vulgarian royalty?" asked the enthusiastic Candide. "You bet, sir!"

Indeed, nothing could have deterred Candide from this unexpected opportunity to socialize with a genuine member of the Vulgarian landed gentry. Freedonia's Founding Fathers had hailed from Vulgaria, and, although the plucky island nation had long ago been engulfed in a sea of European riff-raff, they still spoke Freedonian and they still drank to excess. The two nations shared a special relationship, everyone said so, and the political pundits of both countries seemed quite taken with the catchphrase.

Candide and Wadsworth hopped inside Sir Crampton's limousine without further ado. The night was still young and anything could happen—as we have seen so many times before.

XXV

In Which Sir Crampton Hodnet Gets Rid of the Pain of Being a Man

CANDIDE AND WADSWORTH WERE QUIETLY nibbling their hors d'oeuvres in a penthouse suite atop the most exclusive condominium in Wonton. The evening had begun well enough, but Sir Crampton had been hitting the sauce pretty hard in that typically understated, upper-class Vulgarian way, and he was beginning to fade. He sipped his whiskey and soda, frowning at the ceiling embellished with several thousand square feet of frescoes taken from the Sistine Chapel. The Biedermeier-gilded ormolu clock on his Bohemian crystal mantelpiece chimed twelve times, and a chamber orchestra hidden in the shadows of a distant alcove segued into a slinky Boccherini fandango.

"Are you kidding? Live music?" said Candide. "I thought it was the radio playing all this time."

"It's bollocks," replied Sir Crampton. "It sounds like a convocation of sodomitic organ grinders' monkeys frottaging each other's testicles with a cheese grater."

"And your accent's so cool," continued Candide, "you sound like a butler on a TV show."

"I picked up on that, too," said Wadsworth, not to be outdone.

Sir Crampton sighed noisily and tossed the remains of his Turkish Sobranie cigarette into the flames of the solid platinum, nuclear-powered Swiss fireplace.

"If I had the money to do it all over again, I'd have the money to do it all over again," he mumbled. "Frankly, I'm so filthy rich that money makes me feel ... filthy."

"I bet a lot of people would like to know how filthy you can feel about money," replied Candide.

"Oh, I am an exceptionally sordid person," replied Sir Crampton. "Whenever I see or even think upon a large sum of money, I spontaneously ejaculate. My trousers are disgusting. My dry cleaning bills are scandalous."

Wadsworth had been examining the priceless

collection of Old Master oil paintings hanging on the walls around them. A Van Dyke *grisaille* study of several Cavalier King Charles Spaniels playing whist with a topless Nell Gwynne had caught his eye.

"This is really something. Come over here and take a look at this, Candide."

"Gee, that's a beautiful painting you got there, Sir Crampton," said Candide.

"It's almost but not quite entirely the precise opposite of a beautiful painting," sniffed Sir Crampton. "It's visual sewage spewed onto a hapless, undeserving canvas by a slack-jawed, hollow-eyed coprophiliac. I've seen better work on the floor of an uncleaned Turkish toilet."

This reminded Candide that he needed to go to the washroom. Sir Crampton directed him toward a vaulted complex of marble chambers modeled upon the infamous love grottoes of ancient Pompeii. The voluptuous nude sybarites playing the roles of imperial Roman bathhouse attendants lent it all an extra and quite unexpected touch of historical verisimilitude.

"Hey, those girls are freaks," said Candide when he returned. "I can't speak Wontonese, but I think they wanted to lick my entire body dry after I washed my hands."

"They're joyless trollops, the festering, diseased minions of a vile oriental cult sworn to reduce our occidental sex organs into a fetid, colloidal syrup. The smooth brown bodies and exquisite, perfect features are just a sluttish front for their wily, orgasmic guiles."

Candide was rather nonplussed by this. "Trouble, huh? You make it sound kind of appealing, but I'll take your word for it."

"Apart from the forcible organ donations and legalized *droit de seigneur,* the Wontonese have little to offer to the wealthy Anglo-Saxon expatriate," muttered the Vulgarian.

But Wadsworth was on top of things, as usual. He had been examining some of the books lining the polished oak shelves of Sir Crampton's personal library. He pulled out a volume at random and was surprised to discover that he was holding a priceless, Moroccan leather-bound first edition of the King James Bible.

"That was Doctor Pangloss's favorite bedtime reading," exclaimed Candide. "He always said it wasn't called the 'Good Book' for nothing."

"In which case, your Doctor Pangloss was as cretinous as his penchant for double negatives suggests," replied Sir Crampton. "It's utter drivel.

If the Bible had been written by a black man it would be universally reviled as a crude relic of the most appalling tribal savagery imaginable. No offense to Mr. Wadsworth, of course."

"None taken," replied Wadsworth. "Organized religion is the white man's burden, and you're welcome to it. It's almost like a hobby with you people, like golfing or wife-swapping, but all at once and more violent."

Sir Crampton snorted at this. "Ah, I see you're a wit as well. Perhaps some other book in my library will better suit your well-oiled sense of black humor?"

Sir Crampton pulled out another first edition from his shelves, a priceless copy of Voltaire's eighteenth-century masterpiece, *Candide.* He tossed it at our young hero who gasped aloud, baffled by the postmodern, metatextual implications of the book's startling title.

"This is so weird. It's like, I'm the hero—of my own story!" he said.

"How delightful for you," replied Sir Crampton as he fixed himself another whiskey and soda. "And how delightful for the reader."

He prodded the young man's shoulder brusquely, spilling his own drink as he did so.

"Your namesake's inane adventures are a dreary reminder of the infinite permutations of our species' congenital imbecility. It's not writing, it's typing, it's a narrative spew of Gallic bile designed to gain the author easier access to the cankerous, vermin-infested talk show hostesses of the eighteenth century."

"Another book about women. Like the Bible, huh?" sniffed Wadsworth.

"And just like a Frenchman, isn't it, inventing the literature of the bloody obvious?" said Sir Crampton.

"Dude, reality check. It's the twenty-first, not the eighteenth century," said Candide. "And if you keep standing in the way of progress, you'll never reach the future. Heck, even progress won't reach the future if you keep it up. And I bet that other Candide would say the exact same thing if he were here."

Sir Crampton was undeterred. He swayed back and forth as he spoke, the contents of his glass sloshing onto his trousers and shoes. "It's all very well to say that the Enlightenment's been under attack since the Garden of Eden, but to thrust a pimply-faced, idiot man-child into the thick of it for comic effect, that was the master stroke of a diabolically evil French genius. Makes me sick."

He vomited his dinner onto a hand-woven, fifteenth-century Aubusson carpet. When he was finished, he lit a fresh cigarette and smiled weakly at the two travelers. Wadsworth was having none of it, though. The cynical cut of Sir Crampton's boozy jib was getting on his nerves.

"It's not Candide's fault that he can't think for himself. No one ever told him to, anyway," snapped Wadsworth.

"Yeah, you're kind of a bummer, man," said Candide. "You have all this money and education and style, but I think that you're really jealous of me because you'll never be a real Freedonian. You'll never be better than best just by thinking you are. And I was being polite when I said you sounded like a TV butler. You sound more like a fake TV butler!"

The drunken Vulgarian diplomat staggered backwards under the unexpected shock of Candide's stinging accusation. He tottered into a bookcase, flailing his arms wildly to regain his balance as he fell, triggering a cascade of books that tumbled around his ears. One hundred of the greatest classics of world literature pelted his helpless, whiskey-soaked form, a steady avalanche of Petronius, Swift, Lichtenberg, and all their sardonic ilk, each one bound in painfully stiff leather and brass-work covers. The lighter works of more recent centuries followed—Mark Twain and Nathanael West—less dense perhaps, but at higher velocities which culminated in a violent downpour of *The Complete Works of Evelyn Waugh*. The deluge finished with *A Handful of Dust* smashing into the hapless cynic's gin-blossomed nose, precisely equidistant from his watery, reddened eyes. Sir Crampton Hodnet had had enough culture for one night. He ceased struggling and began snoring loudly. The crotch of his trousers glistened suddenly.

Candide and Wadsworth finished their drinks, let themselves out of the penthouse suite, and walked back to their hotel.

"What a weirdo," said Candide. "And who's he trying to impress with his phony enlightenment? That new age double-talk won't even cover his dry-cleaning bills."

Possessed by a sudden pity for his ingenuous though well-meaning friend, Wadsworth clasped Candide's shoulders.

"Don't worry, man. I played Caliban in too

many blaxploitation versions of *The Tempest* to bother anymore with reading between the squirrelly lines of every rich honky pervert who gets his rocks off by not getting his rocks off."

Candide paused for a moment as they stood on the sidewalk outside their hotel. He'd been doing some extra thinking on his own.

"We're leaving Wonton tonight," he informed the startled actor. "This place is a bummer. We're going back to Freedonia. Plus, I need closure from losing Miss Cunegonde. Freedonia's probably got that, too."

XXVI
In Which the Freedonian Body Politic Shakes Its Booty

WADSWORTH THREW THEIR FEW POSSESSIONS into a suitcase while Candide called a cab. The television in their hotel room was tuned to a Wontonese satellite broadcast of the latest political scandal roiling the Freedonian capital of Miltown. The Senate Sub-Committee on Homeland Furnishings was determined to get to the bottom of things, and both Candide and Wadsworth stopped what they were doing to watch the proceedings. It was pretty hot stuff.

The first witness was the Under-Secretary for Faith-Based Emergency Management. "We've been tasked by Congress to follow up on all spontaneous religious 'events,'" he said. "Nothing too complicated, Senator Rex, but, whenever a Muslim suicide child-bomber or an ordained Catholic pederast or even an *ad hoc* Hindu death-mob rears its ugly head, we go in afterwards and make sure that no one gets the wrong idea about god's final solution for themselves and their loved ones. Our mandate is simple: feeling better about feeling really, really bad."

The second witness nodded eagerly. As the Assistant Under-Secretary for Carpal Tunnel Syndrome, he was eager to put his own two cents in.

"I'd like to point out that a lot of these injuries are completely avoidable," he announced. "Chronic wrist and finger pain after these sort of faith-based 'events' is usually the result of excessive onanism on the part of a demoralized and dispirited populace."

He then placed his hand over his microphone and winked in a conspiratorial manner at the Senator. "Bunch of jerk-offs, really," he chuckled *sotto voce*.

That was the wrong tack to take with a three hundred pound, silver-backed stud gorilla. Senator Rex sprang to his feet, shrieking loudly and hurling documents and orange peels at the startled Under-Secretary. The Senator was rumored to run his committee with an iron fist, and he certainly wasn't going to allow these nationally-televised hearings to degenerate into a backslapping concatenation of off-color jokes and sleazy locker room bonhomie.

A fashionably unshaven man dressed in a porkpie hat, skin-tight T-shirt and artfully torn blue jeans cleared his throat. A gasp of recognition swept the crowded room, and dozens of cameras flashed and whirred as the world's best-branded rock-star-cum-philanthropist-philosopher, Star Lee, addressed the committee. His media narrative of vertically integrated global harmony was very much in the air, and his cult demographics were already legendary in the business.

"Why can't we just call onanism by its real name?" rasped Star Lee in his thick Irish brogue. "It's called 'jerking off,' and it wouldn't be necessary if we all learned to love one another instead of just ourselves." He ran his fingers through his bronzed, windswept hair and smiled at a goggle-eyed stenographer. "That's why I'm working with my African friend, President Foufou, to help impoverished Savoyards rebuild their war-ravaged numerical system by using their own bling resources. Together, we're creating a new world where every man and woman counts—"

The infuriated Senator Rex leaped onto the table and scuttled across it until he was face to face with the startled rock star. Curling back his lips to reveal his massive canines, the Senator snatched Star Lee's microphone and furiously humped it. The abrupt squeal of grotesquely viscous feedback filled the room.

"Be that as it may," boomed another witness, a crew-cut, medal-bedecked four-star Army general, "but impoverished Third World slums and *favelas* such as Mr. Star Lee just alluded to are notorious breeding grounds for anti-Freedonian terrorism. Keep 'em onanist, I say. Ultimately, every spilled Savoyard seed is another Freedonian fighting man or woman who will get back home sufficiently alive to stimulate the economy enough to support the Defense Department's budget."

"That's so true," said Candide to Wadsworth. "If it wasn't for us veterans, there wouldn't be any more veterans."

A doughy-faced, ageless man in a nondescript business suit leaned over to speak into the general's microphone. "In fact, at Baron Incorporated we've developed a new generation of militarized fungibles that can take out a Third World economy within ten minutes post-launch. Our military quants have also come up with some top secret algorithms that establish a triple-A credit rating for Third World rubble and corpses so rapidly that they automatically qualify for reconstruction loans from our post-invasion finance teams before the first Freedonian troops even hit the ground. The synergy is incredible—when you walk into a room where people are doing this stuff, it just overwhelms you."

"That's amazing," said the general, impressed by Baron Incorporated's forward thinking on the subject. Senator Rex yipped his own cautious approval of this encouraging development.

"Thanks, General," said the man from Baron Incorporated.

"It just goes to show," said Candide, "that the entire Baron family can be dead or sexually unavailable but the name of Baron Incorporated lives on. As long as Freedonia's enemies have the presence of mind to read the logo on the missiles aimed at them, naturally."

"If they can read, of course," chuckled Wadsworth.

"And if they have the time," added Candide. "Those things are darn fast on the homestretch."

Senator Rex reared up on his hind legs and barked a warning to his staff. They dove for cover while their boss tagged the Senate press pool with a jet of hot urine. The blurred, chaotic scene on the television screen abruptly cut to a commercial.

An attractive woman in a bathing suit was looking into a crystal ball. She looked up at the camera, clearly surprised. "If you're like most people, your life is probably in quite a fog by now. But guess what? The Psychic Hotline already knows that—and even more!"

Her bathing suit changed into a business suit and a few dollar bills fluttered down upon her shoulders in a desultory manner. "Call today and discover ... money ... romance ... happiness ... before someone less deserving than you gets it all."

Candide dialed the number on the television screen. "This might be my last chance to find Miss Cunegonde," he sighed.

"I played a TV psychic in a sitcom pilot about the bumper cults of the seventies," warned Wadsworth, "and I never saw it coming, none of it: the poisoned Kool-Aid, the random sniper attacks, the cover photo on *Rolling Stone*—"

Candide motioned Wadsworth to be quiet, he had gotten through to the Psychic Hotline.

"Can you tell me if I'll ever find true love?" he asked.

"Mr. Candide, is that you?" replied the psychic. His foreign accent was vaguely familiar.

"How did you know my name?" replied the perplexed young Freedonian. "Only a real psychic would know who I am before I tell them."

"As always, you are correct, Mr. Candide," said the excited psychic. "Can you not guess? It is I, your personal assistant Sanjay!"

"Sanjay? You're a psychic? Dude, that's awesome!" exclaimed Candide.

"The vagaries of human destiny are an open book to me, Mr. Candide. And I already have some good news for you. I've found Miss Cunegonde!"

XXVII
In Which Everyone
Gets with the Plan

THE EBULLIENT SANJAY HAD MUCH TO SAY. "I never reached Wollyhood. I was detained by Freedonian Immigration and deported back to my paternal uncle's tea stall in Funkidesh. It is a modest family business which also doubles as a major nerve center in the international psychic hotline industry. All of Funkidesh is dabbling in this business right now. It is a natural fit between one billion congenitally gabby Hindus and five billion credit-worthy lonely hearts."

"Heck, Sanjay, only a natural-born entrepreneur like you could even hope to beat those odds," admitted Candide.

But Sanjay had more news. "However, I sense that Miss Cunegonde's deed of trust has been sold to a tall, dark stranger from Baron Incorporated. He has influenced her into temping with Bon-Temps®, their escort agency subsidiary in Miltown. I discern the inauspicious spiritual and physical influence of many Congressmen and lobbyists upon her."

"Right on, Miss Cunegonde," said Wadsworth, who had been listening in on the speakerphone. "Screwing the guys who are screwing Freedonia."

Sanjay was not so optimistic, though. "Unfortunately, her cosmic avatar has become bloated with carnal misuse and pharmaceutical excess. Her features have coarsened, as have her breasts, buttocks, and thighs. I also detect a major karmic pattern of lesbianism with a minor chakra of impromptu videography. She is festooned with many tattoos, but I am unable to discern their precise message as yet."

Candide was having none of this defeatist psychic talk. "Now hold on, Sanjay. I'm an orphan, an Army deserter, a suspected terrorist, and a multiple murderer, but I'm also a good old Freedonian country boy and I'm standing by my girl—hell yeah!"

As usual, Wadsworth had already come up

with a better plan. "Why don't you wire Sanjay the cash for his airfare to Miltown? We can meet him there and rescue Miss Cunegonde together."

"Awesome plan, Wadsworth," said Candide. "And thanks, Sanjay, for always being in the right place at the right time. I love what you do, man."

If this narrative had been produced by the usual cabal of literary illuminati who have dominated the bestseller lists since the late eighteenth century, one could now expect a lengthy explanation of how society made Miss Cunegonde into what she is today. But this is not the eighteenth century. It is the twenty-first century, a century of personal choice, and modern Freedonian youth have personally chosen to have nothing meaningful to do with one another. The no-strings sexual hook-up is the coin of their commodified realm, and Miss Cunegonde's puzzling sexual appeal was carnal proof of Gresham's Law, an economist's maxim that reminds us that bad money drives out good.

Perhaps Sanjay had guessed correctly, perhaps Candide's sweetheart had indeed declined into a perspiring, obese, bleached blonde squeezed into skin-tight spandex sausage casings, liberally tattooed, well-armed with startlingly second-hand features, and a slurring penchant for drugged potty talk—in short, sexual pop culture dynamite. No matter! Candide's summation of the entire business was a splendid example of the Freedonian penchant to apply consumerism to all facets of the human condition.

"Hey, my girl's a big-time escort-temp. Kind of a turn-on, huh?" said Candide, as he and Wadsworth greeted Sanjay in the arrival lounge of the Miltown airport.

"Quite so, Mr. Candide," replied Sanjay. "I sense that at this very moment Miss Cunegonde's *kundalini* is moving some critical legislation through the Freedonian Congress before it is detected by the common electorate."

"Let's head for the Congress right now," said Candide. "I'm still pretty rich, and I'm sure we can work something out with these tall, dark, stranger Congressmen or whatever they call themselves."

Candide and his companions followed the signs to the nearest taxi stand, navigating their way through the crowded airport terminal until they were intercepted by two gaunt men wearing shabby white robes and cheap flip-flops. One of the men thrust a few wilted flowers at Candide while the other began hopping spasmodically from foot to foot while shaking a small handbell and waving his palsied arms in the air.

"Would you like to make a voluntary offering?" said the man with the flowers, waving a tin cup at Candide. "Deprogramming is expensive and not covered by most insurance plans. Did you know that together we can make a difference?"

"We're in a hurry right now," replied Candide, "and besides, too much of anything, even difference, is harmful. You should put on regular clothes if you want people to give you their money."

"We're all a bit different," said the man, "and rightly so, because god made us just the way we are."

"And that's why it's better to be just a little bit different by being even more the same," replied Candide. "Heck, everybody knows that. That's why it's called freedom."

"Good lord," exclaimed the man, "it's Candide!"

"Is that you, Doctor Pangloss?" exclaimed Candide.

"Is that Candide?" asked the other man in mid-hop.

"And what are you doing with Junior Baron?" asked Candide. "Aren't both of you dead?"

The Doctor and Junior Baron's bloodshot eyes blinked spasmodically in the harsh fluorescent lights of the airport terminal. Their shaven skulls and tattered, dirty robes were silent proof of the depths to which they had fallen.

"Being dead might be an improvement upon our current situation," sighed the Doctor. He listlessly shook his empty tin cup. "We thought that joining The Plan would be a step up, but it's proved pretty disappointing so far, I have to admit."

"The Plan? What's that?" asked Wadsworth. "One of those hippy cults that white folks are always joining whenever they make eye contact with some freak on the subway?"

"Let me answer this question, Doctor Pangloss," interrupted Junior Baron. "OK, first of all, I'll forget that you tried to kill me, Candide. I've learned a lot of spiritual truths since then and luckily for you, revenge isn't one of them."

"Right on, right on," murmured Doctor Pangloss. Junior Baron glared at his companion, and the Doctor fell silent.

"Just don't do it again. Second, it's not a cult,

it's more like an HMO except that we manage health care by removing the problem instead of just solving the problem like other, less enlightened health insurance cults do."

"Exercise freaks are stressing out our health care system," added Doctor Pangloss. "It's always me-me-me with these self-absorbed fitness nuts. Sure, we need affordable health care for all Freedonians, but does it really make sense to care for the healthy? That, my dear Candide, is what they call an oxymoron."

"Gesundheit," replied his former student.

"Yeah, I see it," said Wadsworth. "They're physically fit, but, mentally, it's all a set-up. So how's the panhandling come into it?"

"I'm not really sure," admitted the Doctor. "I glanced at a pamphlet about The Plan that someone gave me on the subway, hoping to learn how to combat this pagan cult which was corrupting the Christian youth of Freedonia, and I guess I just, uh, got accidentally converted."

"It's simple," said Junior Baron. "The more money we collect for The Plan, the less money there is for everybody else in the economy to get stressed over. According to The Plan, the number one cause of workplace injuries in the executive suite is worker salaries. How do you think that feels to a health insurance executive who's just trying to make ends meet at the end of the day?"

"I think we should go now," interrupted Doctor Pangloss. "Here comes our supervisor."

A large, muscular and far better nourished man in a tracksuit was running toward them, waving his arms. The Doctor and Junior tossed their tin cup, handbell, and nosegay into the nearest trash bin and raced toward the exit.

"Those two assholes are in big trouble," sputtered the man when he reached Candide and Wadsworth. "I just caught one of them jerking off next to the full-body scanners in the security zone, and now they're talking trash to tourists."

"Chill out, man," said Wadsworth. "It's a free country."

The man glared at Wadsworth. "What are you, some kind of smart ass? Just because Freedonia has the word 'free' in it doesn't mean it is."

"That still doesn't make it not free," replied Wadsworth.

The man clenched his beefy fists. "If you were a real Freedonian, you'd know that better than best is never free. It's pretty damn expensive, otherwise everybody would have some."

Before the baffled Wadsworth could reply to this, a cloud of dollar bills exploded around them. The quick-thinking Sanjay had tossed the contents of his wallet into the air, and the airport terminal was magically transformed into a noisy bedlam of people shoving and pushing at each other to get at this sudden windfall.

"The maya of something for nothing is particularly fleeting," shouted Sanjay above the din. "This brutish acolyte of The Plan will soon regain his ill-mannered senses and resume menacing us. A hasty exit is indicated."

They ran outside and found Junior and the Doctor struggling with the door of a taxi whose driver seemed loathe to let them into his cab. Candide waved a fistful of twenty-dollar bills at the man, and all five men hastily piled into the vehicle.

"Take us to the Congress of the United States of Freedonia," ordered Candide. "And step on it. We're on a mission of love, so screw defensive driving."

And off they sped into the rush hour traffic of Miltown.

XXVIII

How Doctor Pangloss and Junior Baron Expunged Their Debts to Society

THE NOTORIOUSLY CONGESTED TRAFFIC OF THE Freedonian capital gave Candide ample time to discover what his tutor and childhood companion had both been up to recently. "So, Doctor Pangloss, being questioned to death by anti-terrorism experts must have hurt pretty bad."

"Luckily for me, they weren't better than best, Freedonian anti-terrorism experts," replied the Doctor, "they were just your average, Joe Six-pack Freedonian sadists masquerading as highly-trained, Freedonian anti-terrorism experts. When they pushed that fluorescent light bulb into my rectum, that's when I knew I was going to be OK. Fluoride is the greatest single case of scientific fraud in this century. All those dummies did was deplete the brainpower of my lower intestines, the exact place where my brain and all its so-called facts were least likely to be found."

"That's nothing," sniffed Junior. "After being kicked flat by Candide and then partially re-inflating myself with a can of compressed air, I flagged down an ambulance. Without my wallet, they could only take me as far as the nearest veterinarian clinic. Of course, Daddy always said that the smartest way to get rich was to use other people's money, so after they pumped me full of helium at the clinic, I stole the janitor's wallet and struck out on my own."

"Only in Freedonia," chuckled Candide.

But Doctor Pangloss wasn't finished. "A Costaguanan helicopter pilot was supposed to drop my dead body into the ocean, but, thanks to his slacker Latino work ethic and inflated tropical libido, I was tossed into a hotel swimming pool full of naked hookers and drunken businessmen. The steamy mixture of gin sweat, bodily fluids, and chlorinated water re-ionized my depleted synapses and neutrons, and I was able to escape the tropical slut-pool under my own power. Climate change scientists will deny that anything like that could ever happen but just google it for yourself. You'll see."

Junior glared at him. "All right, I'll admit that posing as a janitor who happened to be trading animal tranquilizers for sex with underage high school cheerleaders was a tough sell legally, but socially, it really opened some doors for me. Prison was one of those doors. Sure, no one is tougher on crime than criminals, but statistically I was still safer behind bars, especially when the majority of successful Freedonian criminals happen to wear three-piece suits and work nine to five. As soon as I got out, I skipped straight to the bottom of the career ladder to maximize my potential vertical momentum. They don't teach you that kind of thing in business school, I can tell you."

"Nobody bounces faster and harder than a Freedonian," agreed the Doctor. "I should know because I laid low in the Costaguanan jungle for six weeks, posing as a rain forest jungle macaque exhibiting simple tool-making abilities such as bumming cigarettes and spare change from Freedonian eco-tourists."

"What about the evolution weirdoes?" asked Candide. "Didn't they freak out when they saw you evolving backwards?"

The Doctor chuckled at this. "You bet, son. Just one naked, dirty, white guy panhandling from a tree can put god back into anybody's so-called theories. But as I was saying, a rich and childless couple from New Shazzizle decided to adopt me and bring me back with them to their swank apartment on the Upper West Side. For the next few months, I ate, slept, and regained my strength, confining my animal activities to fooling around on the internet whenever Mr. and Mrs. Kreplach went out. That's how I hooked up with Earl, a transvestite who was impersonating a cop in various online chat rooms as part of her master's thesis in performance art."

"Modern art, huh?" interrupted Wadsworth. "It's all fake. It's not even acting. When the cameras are rolling, I only have to fake being a fake, not actually be one."

Junior snorted loudly. "OK then, smart ass, try faking life as an ex-con with a pancake physique and an expired MBA. But hey, I still got game. I began taking night classes, saved up to buy a car, got myself permanently re-inflated, and started dating again. Then one day I walked off the street and into the lobby of the biggest Fortune 500 company in Freedonia. I talked my way past the security guards, secretaries, the HR drones, all the way to the CEO's office. With just a piece of paper and a number two pencil, I showed him how he could save millions by making every one of his employees start over at the bottom, except for himself, of course."

"You just walked right into The Man's office?" asked Wadsworth.

"Yeah, what a jerk," said Junior. "He had security throw me out and then stole my idea. I didn't make a dime out of it, but a few weeks later, I spit into his hamburger when I recognized him in the line-up at my drive-through window. He pretended to recognize me in the surveillance camera footage, but my court-appointed attorney got me referred to a state mental hospital for observation. Of course, the entire time they thought they were observing me, *I was observing them.*"

The Doctor sighed loudly. "If only it were that easy. It turns out that my new friend Earl was really a cop pretending to be a transvestite performance artist pretending to be a cop. And his thesis presentation was a videotape of my perp walk, indictment, and conviction for felony internet lewdness."

The baffled Candide scratched his head.

"Who would have guessed that the punishment for being lewd is having to spend even more time with lewd people?"

Doctor Pangloss shrugged. "More government red tape and burdensome regulations like that certainly isn't the answer. But once I got out on parole, I cut back on the casual sex with strangers and the prescription drug abuse and joined a cult instead. That color brochure was pretty persuasive."

"Yeah, whatever," said Junior. "When I got out on parole, my freshly-minted crazy person skills were red hot. I started out with The Plan in an entry-level position, making eye contact with other white people on the subway, and, after a few weeks of that, they promoted me to airport greeter."

Junior paused, staring pointedly at Candide. "And I'd like to know why my slacker sister is temp-escorting in an oak-paneled, air-conditioned congressman's penthouse office suite while I have to bust my ass hustling shekels off argumentative rubes in the economy class arrivals lounge at the airport."

Doctor Pangloss was more sanguine about their situation. "Don't play into the media's hands,

Junior. They love playing the blame game, especially in airport washrooms or highway rest stops. Just accept the fact that 'IN GOD WE TRUST' is the only excuse you'll ever need."

"That and finding Miss Cunegonde before it's too late," said Candide. And just in time, too, for they had arrived at the front doors of the Freedonian Congress.

XXIX
How Candide Rocked a Senate

THE FREEDONIAN LEGISLATURE WAS DEBATING federal monetary policy at that very moment so our hero's arrival on the floor of the Senate went unremarked by everyone.

"Replacing the Freedonian 'greenback' with this proposed 'wetback' will both expunge the national debt and solve our illegal immigration problems forever," announced a Senator to his restive colleagues.

Another Senator leaped to his feet. "Perhaps my learned colleague has forgotten that illegal immigration is illegal and that replacing 'greenbacks' with 'wetbacks' would make our legal tender into illegal tender? That's crazy!"

"They're immigrants, they're always on the

move, darn 'em," said another Senator. "The sneaky fellows wouldn't stay put in our wallets or pocketbooks for a moment. Plus the word 'wetback,' it's going to look funny on money orders and checks, especially those customized ones with puppies and horses and flags printed on them."

An uproar ensued. Senators shouted at each other, sheafs of paper were tossed into the air, lapels were grabbed, and total chaos threatened to engulf the entire legislative branch of the Freedonian system of government. Candide had had enough. He leaped atop the nearest desk.

"Hey, get a grip, Senator dudes," he shouted. "We only want you to make laws because we don't trust each other, not because we like them. Or you."

The chamber fell silent, the Senators stared in amazement at this brash young man.

"Talking sense may be a lost cause but so is talking nonsense," continued Candide. "You can't control the out-of-control borders of this great nation by squeezing every darn illegal alien into every darn ATM in the land, at least not until you start listening to your gut and stop listening to experts. But you might want to start by listening to me, because I'm an expert—in love!"

Candide's audience gasped loudly, and several

Senators ducked beneath their desks for cover. Candide slapped his muscular abdomen proudly.

"I've learned more about love from eighteen years with my gut than I could have learned in a lifetime of going to college. Some folks say it's the heart that matters in these things, but, like I said already, stop listening to those so-called experts. Here's what my gut says to me: I see you and I love you but we cannot do anything about it. So let's get it on with Miss Cunegonde instead."

Candide paused to wipe a tear from his eye. This was harder than he thought it would be. His sudden outburst had surprised even himself. Sensing danger, Doctor Pangloss took over.

"Love propelled this gutsy young Freedonian atop this desk," said the Doctor. "And it's keeping him there despite all your wealthy special interests and K Street lobbyists and clean-cut, young male interns. Heck, even gravity can't beat this kind of love. That's because there's a split-level Colonial with a white picket fence and an ovary full of fresh-faced young kids waiting somewhere in this building for my young friend and her name is Miss Cunegonde."

A small, aged Macarenan woman in a faded tube top and hot pants pushed her way through the Senators. "Horny gringos always talk about other people's ovaries when the going gets tough," announced the old woman. "But when you've lost as many ovaries as I have, you know that nothing lasts forever, especially cheap tits and pretty-doll looks. Here's your Miss Cunegonde, Candide. How do you like her now?"

The old woman cackled as Miss Cunegonde appeared behind her, simpering coyly at the wealthy old men crowding around her. Sanjay's grim predictions were correct, the young woman had faded and enlarged at the same time. Some of the healthier Senators smiled back at her pneumatic breasts.

"Oh, hey … wow … whassup?" said Miss Cunegonde to Candide.

"Just hanging out," replied Candide. "Chilling."

"You really came back for me, huh? Bitching. It's like you're still in that frigging movie from before, but it's a real-life movie now. Awesome."

A doughy-faced, ageless man in a nondescript business suit stepped forward and shook Candide's hand. "Good work, Candide. I'm with Baron Incorporated, and I have to tell you that this new love angle of yours is going to look great PR-wise with our emerging female market."

He leaned toward Candide and lowered his voice. "It fits in perfectly with our Pink-Oh® guerrilla marketing push. If we can get the ladies to purchase weapons systems the way they buy shoes and diet pills, well, I think you get the picture."

"You like my shoes?" giggled Miss Cunegonde. "Senator Rex said that they're perpetual beta."

The man from Baron Incorporated ignored this. "Of course, Senator Rex has been a significant investor in Miss Cunegonde, but I'm sure we can work something out with him. Since she's technically both the CEO and the property of Baron Incorporated, she can sign herself over to you. Just send us a check in the mail."

"This is total bullshit," shouted Junior Baron. "I still own fifty percent of Baron Incorporated, and I'm not letting the other fifty percent go to my dumb-ass sister and her white trash boyfriend. The day that stupid people can get filthy rich is the day that Freedonia is completely screwed!"

The man from Baron Incorporated reached toward Junior and flicked a piece of lint off his shoulder. Junior convulsed suddenly and fell to the floor.

"You kids go and have a great life," said the man to Candide and Miss Cunegonde. "And don't forget the check, OK?" The man dragged the moaning Junior Baron toward the men's washroom of the Freedonian Senate. The door opened, and Candide glimpsed a man bent over a washstand, a man in a perfectly tailored suit who might have been Sir Crampton Hodnet or Mister Chad or perhaps even the President of Savoy. In the shadows behind the man, an immense simian shape crouched atop a urinal, gibbering madly and pawing at itself as it watched the writhing form of the hapless Junior Baron being dragged across the floor toward it.

There was a horrible shriek, the washroom door slammed shut, and it was over. Candide turned away, shaken by this unexpected glimpse into the halls of power.

XXX
How the Enlightenment Got Its Groove Back

FLEEING NORTHWARDS WAS THE OLD WOMAN'S idea. It had always been her favorite direction anyway. The indispensable Sanjay hotwired Senator Rex's Humvee, and, while he and Wadsworth took turns driving, the old woman had a frank talk with Candide.

"Miss Cunegonde's better off with me," she told him. "She's ugly now, and you've always been stupid; but I didn't survive being a farmer's daughter from the poorest state in Macarena by keeping my only remaining, unsold eye closed whenever I got screwed. You call it lesbianism, but Miss Cunegonde and I call it a vacation from having to sleep with men so witless that they'll pay for fake love and boast about it afterwards."

"Miss Cunegonde and I already talked it over," replied Candide, "and we're planning to have one of those plutonic relationships. There's plenty of her to go around anyway, so help yourself."

"Sounds like a self-serve, cracker barrel love buffet to me," chuckled Wadsworth.

"Do not belittle the faded blonde kismet of Mr. Candide's sexual karma," warned Sanjay. "The combined *kundalinis* of Miss Cunegonde and the old woman promise a substantial carnal nirvana for all of our late-night chakras." The young Hindu glanced furtively at Miss Cunegonde, who smiled back at him.

They continued driving north. They soon left Freedonia behind them, and the multi-lane highway narrowed into a rutted dirt road winding through the endless boreal forests of Canada. It began snowing, a few flurries at first and then an interminable blizzard that forced them to stop and take shelter in a rusting Quonset hut surrounded by ramshackle mobile homes and collapsing tool sheds. This was the village of Saint-Arpenteur-des-Neiges. They could go no further. The road had simply ceased to exist.

It continued snowing. Candide purchased the Quonset hut with the last of Ben and Gerry's money. Wadsworth, who had once played a black handyman in an interracial porno video, soon made the place warm and habitable.

It snowed harder. Miss Cunegonde and the old woman entertained their desultory rural clients on the salvaged seat of an abandoned logging truck. When business was slow, they entertained each other. Sanjay improvised an indoor marijuana grow-op with the runway beacon lights he had purloined from a nearby emergency airfield. Doctor Pangloss and Candide busied themselves watering and pruning their valuable crop—Candide took to wearing bib overalls and dipping snuff while the Doctor took to packing heat. Wadsworth played the essential role of a big-city drug dealer come to show the country pot heads a thing or two. At least I'm acting, he told his agent on the telephone.

It was snowing even harder when Paco appeared one evening, exhausted by his dangerous trek through the uninhabited forests.

"Jesus and I walked all the way from Wonton," he explained, "hand in hand for thousands of miles, hopping from ice floe to ice floe until he was mauled to death by an angry flash mob of radio-controlled polar bears, just south of what used to be the polar ice cap. It was terrifying, they came out of nowhere. There was so much blood and screaming, I think I may have been born again."

It was still snowing a few months later when a Canadian government social worker came by to check up on them. "How are you folks settling in?" she asked. "It must be quite a change from living in Freedonia, eh?"

"Man, it's like ... my paranoia has no focus anymore," replied Candide. "For instance, we're all sitting here, and there's a nuke. How would I know which wire to cut?"

"You mean, like, you've got the red wire and the green wire," said Wadsworth, "and we're both sweating and you're like, I don't know, I'm going to go with my gut feeling even though I'm color blind from jerking off all the time?"

"Hey, shithead, my boyfriend is a frigging army man," snapped Miss Cunegonde. "He kills people with his bare hands, asshole. And he doesn't need to jerk off because those are the very same hands he uses to make hot, sweaty, filthy animal love to me every night ... bitch."

"Government social worker, is that even a job?" asked Doctor Pangloss. "I'm just noting the timing here ... an admitted socialist asking a lot of personal questions while poking around in the middle of a forest which isn't even supposed to be here."

"Yeah, are you making it up as you go along?" asked Paco. "Because in Isaiah 49:16, Jesus—who had the same name as the only man who ever loved me—he says, 'I wrote your name on the palm of my hand to remember you.' And now you're disrespecting the hands of every Jesus who loved me enough to write me down ... skank."

"My friends, cease this fruitless agitation of barren mantras," pleaded Sanjay. "You must shed the destructive psychic karma of your previous Freedonian incarnations if you wish to be at peace with being at peace. Embrace your inner chakras and learn to unwind your maya."

"Such crap," snarled the old woman. "Being an old woman without even a left leg left to stand on is a piss-ant compared to being a gringo so stupid that he doesn't know how easy he has it by just having to be stupid all the time. Paranoia's a luxury when you've been stripped buck naked to drink codeine cough syrup from a broken bottle in a cattle truck packed with a dozen farmers who are used to doing it with goats. Hell, just wearing clothes is a luxury for a Macarenan whore like me. At least in Canada a single woman can fall asleep on a bus without getting pregnant."

Shaking her head in dismay, the government social worker gave Candide a carton of sedatives and another carton of mental health pamphlets. She drove off on her snowmobile and never returned. She was not missed.

It continued snowing, even harder now. There was no end to this snow, it was a natural phenomenon of such epic proportions that it defied all description and beggared the imagination. Of course, this was perfectly normal behavior for any self-respecting natural phenomenon, especially in light of humanity's perpetual refusal to get the message. For countless millennia, the immensity of nature's indifference to us has served as a final, irrefutable verdict upon the human condition, and for countless millennia, no one seems to have truly grasped the overwhelmingly obvious point of it all. How much longer until we get it? And when we do, then what?

Fortunately for this author, there are other, far better authors who have waxed rhapsodic over such natural phenomena and their philosophical implications, authors who must remain anonymous, for in this, the better than best of all possible worlds, it's simply not sporting to expect one's readers to remember every scribbler that crosses their path. They have better things to do, probably better than best things to do.

Which is why it continued snowing even harder now. Indeed, the young Candide watched sleepily the flakes, silver and dark, falling obliquely against the fluorescent runway lights of the grow-op. Yes, the internet was right: snow was general all over Canada. It was falling on every part of the boreal forest, on the treeless tundra, on the Canadian Rockies, and, farther eastward, softly falling into the dark mutinous Laurentian waves.

It lay thickly drifted on the crooked trailer homes and crumbling shacks, on the sagging, rusted dome of their Quonset hut, it lay on the forgotten Humvee parked outside, on the barren woods. Candide's soul swooned slowly as he heard the snow falling faintly through the universe and faintly falling, like the descent of their last end, upon the unseen Rapture drone orbiting high above him, spying through the window of the Quonset hut to see our hero laboring on his hands and knees in his sweltering, narcotic jungle.

In a windowless, soundproofed room a thousand miles away, a man in an anonymous military uniform stared at the flickering surveillance image of Candide on his video monitor.

It's that guy from the Funkistani potato farm suicide bombing, he thought. *What a dope.*

The man pressed a button on his keyboard, and Candide vanished. The monochrome image of a moonlit Amazonian jungle clearing took his place on the monitor. A dozen half-naked men, women, and children were sleeping on the bare earth, huddled around a dwindling fire. Their few communal, Stone Age possessions lay strewn about them.

Hippy rich kids slumming, thought the man. *The chick's kind of hot, though ... underneath the dirt.*

He fiddled with a joystick, and the drone's camera zoomed into the shadowy edges of the forest clearing. A jungle macaque had twisted some twigs into a crude hand blender and was fixing itself a mojito with the hallucinogenic yagé it had siphoned from a stolen calabash.

Candide lit a joint and inhaled deeply.

As soon as we sell all this dope, he thought, *I'm buying a home security system, one of those pro-active ones from Baron Incorporated, the ones that can read an intruder's thoughts before he even knows he has them. That and stereo headphones so we can tune out the screaming.*

Candide's eyes narrowed as he exhaled. He felt … better than best. He nodded at Doctor Pangloss.

"War on drugs is hell," announced Candide to his friend. "Someone's always trying to rip off your grow-op. They better learn to cultivate their own garden if they know what's good for them."

JACQUES O'BEAN (1961-2011) WAS AN ÉMIGRÉ Costaguanan scholar of American popular culture. His only novel, *Candide en Amérique,* was written for use as a classroom text shortly before his dismissal from the École normale supérieure du Rimouski, Québec. Upon returning to Costaguana, he entered politics as a Falangist (Reformed) congressional candidate in a bitterly fought campaign which culminated in his abduction by a former student who had escaped from a mental hospital. O'Bean's body was never discovered.

MAHENDRA SINGH IS A FREE-LANCE ILLUSTRATOR and author in Montréal.

NB. THE ILLUSTRATION ON PAGE 186 DEPICTS, from left to right, James Mason, Voltaire, David Hume and Georg Christoph Lichtenberg. The young women remain, alas, anonymous.

Also from Rosarium

STORIES A TRIBUTE TO SAMUEL R. DELANY

FOR CHIP

EDITED BY NISI SHAWL AND BILL CAMPBELL

"... an eye-opening illumination of the full reach and depth of Delany's influence."

– New York Times

Featuring the works of Junot Díaz,
Michael Swanwick, Nalo Hopkinson,
Geoff Ryman, Ellen Kushner, Nick Harkaway,
Kit Reed, and more.